VICTEROTICA I

WILDHEART

WILDHEART BOOKS
an imprint of
Oleander Press
16 Orchard Street
Cambridge
CB1 1JT
www.oleanderpress.com

ISBN: 9781909349483
Printed in England

VICTEROTICA I

A CARNAL COLLECTION
(Sex Stories from the Victorian Age)

*Five tales of lust, passion and
deviance from the 19th Century*

WILDHEART

CONTENTS

THE AMATORY EXPERIENCES
OF A SURGEON

James Campbell

Printed for the Nihilists

Moscow – 1881

CHAPTER I

Not all the glowing descriptions of amatory writers, not the inspired breath of passion itself, can truly, and in sufficient degree estimate the force of those desires, and the intoxicating delirium of that enjoyment in which the softer sex plays so important a part, and in the gratification of which it relishes a more than equal degree of pleasure. Were I to cover these pages with descriptions of the most seductive or lascivious scenes, I should fail to realize its full effect.

Language stops short of the reality. No sweeter words, however passionate, however glowing, could transport the bosom, and enthral the frame, like the one magic soul dissolving sensation, experienced by lovers in the celebration of these mystic rites; but if my readers will follow me, while I tell them of some of my amatory experiences, their own feelings may perhaps enable them to sympathise with mine, and thus by analogy, enjoy again some of the most sensual and moving incidents in their own careers.

To say that I was born of respectable parents would, in the full acceptation of the words, be false. My mother was of that disgraced and neglected race, a discarded mistress; my father, a nobleman of the first rank, while still a young man, full of the fiery vices of youth, had caught her eye, his handsome form and noble bearing won her simple love.

The old story followed. He seduced her, kept her awhile to be his toy, and at length, grown tired of her society, threw her off as a plaything of which he was weary. She died, but he lived on to break the heart of many other innocent creatures.

Whatever may have been his errors, among his redeeming points must be reckoned his care of his illegitimate child.

After my mother's death I was sent to a boarding school, and at the age of fourteen had grown a tall, well-made and genteel looking youth. It is needless to say, that it was here, in the society of other lads, many of whom were my seniors, that I was first made acquainted with all that is necessary for men to know in a theoretical point of view; of practice with the opposite sex, I knew nothing, but my ardent imagination pictured ecstasies, which fell but little short of the reality, and which was further assisted in its expanded ideas by the scenes we boys enacted among ourselves. All that we could do we did, and we gave each other as much amusement, as we knew how to administer.

It was no uncommon thing for us to wander into other boys' beds, and each taking in his hand the warm, half stiffened little member of the other, to produce by pleasing friction, that overflow which, feeble substitute as it was, caused us so much enjoyment.

Often too, would one of the bigger boys wantonly insert his glowing affair within the lips of some fair-haired youngster, and there lie and permit himself to be titillated in the most agreeable manner possible.

3

These pastimes were so common that we scarcely ever passed a night without the repetition of some of them.

I was not fully initiated into all the mysterious practices of the elder boys till my sixteenth birthday, when they admitted me as a member of the upper-class, as all above that age styled themselves. Their custom was that each lad on attaining the age of sixteen had to give the upper-class a banquet, to inaugurate his admission amongst their privileged circle.

My particular chum, Bob Ferguson, had for some time whispered to me when he played with my prick, that there was a great surprise in store for me on my birthday.

Well, at last the momentous night arrived, and being the best provided boy in the school, (as to pocket-money), thanks to the liberality of my father, we had a really splendid banquet, which they all declared quite eclipsed any previous affair of the sort.

On those occasions our master, usually a strict disciplinarian, generally gave us permission to enjoy ourselves, and make as much noise, or have what fun we liked in the big boys' room. Little could he have ever dreamed of the excesses that were actually enacted at these birthday feasts.

After stuffing ourselves with cold game-pie, tarts, and champagne, the real business of my installation commenced by all stripping off their clothes.

Even now my soul thrills as I recall to mind that room full of handsome naked youths, several of them as handsome as Adonis himself, some of the eldest having quite a beautiful growth of silky hair ornamenting their pricks, and my readers may be sure that inflamed as we were with feasting and wine, the sight of each other's charms made everyone rampant and ready for action.

A couple of them now began to handle my tool, gently frigging and pulling back the foreskin as they passed their hands up and down the stiffened shaft; next they proceeded to anoint it with some pomade, and one of the biggest boys presenting his bottom as he stooped forward on a chair, they made me shove into him, till I was fairly in. The delicious warmth of the tight sheath which held me was so exciting, that without further instructions I fucked him as naturally as possible, clinging tightly to him with my arms, and thoroughly enjoying it.

Presently the captain of the class, a fine, handsome youth of eighteen, attacked me in the rear, but being well lubricated, although the pricking pain attending his first insertion was rather sharp, he was soon in full possession, and my double position of fucker and fuckee soon drove me almost mad with delight. I seemed to spend my juice again and again every time; he delighted me with his warm overflow in my bottom. At last I fairly fainted from excess of emotion and when I came to myself found I was lying on one of the beds with Bob Ferguson's cock in my mouth, whilst the captain was deliciously sucking my reinvigorated tool.

What an orgy of lust we enacted that night! It seemed to me heavenly at the time, and even now as I write these lines my old cock stands at the remembrance of it.

Soon after this I left school, preparatory to commencing the career of life, which had been marked out for me; but after a while, finding the occupation of dispensing medicine too irksome, I obtained the permission of my noble parent to study for the medical profession.

Accordingly I went to London, and after several years studious application at the hospitals, I received my diploma from the Examiners at Surgeon's Hall, or in modern parlance, from the Royal College of Surgeons.

A short time after that I settled in a small practice, at the village near which my paternal patron had his principal estate.

It is needless to say that our relationship was kept as secret as the envious gossips of the place could reasonably desire; all they knew was that Lord L— had extended his patronage to me, and that was enough to excite the jealousy of the tuft-hunters of the neighborhood.

Notwithstanding these ill-natured people however, my lord's patronage was quite sufficient to bring me plenty of practice, and within a time I became the fashionable doctor of the district.

This was not entirely owing to the reasons, cogent as they were, which I have above detailed; to a very natural desire to succeed, and to attention to my patients, combined, I flatter myself, with no mean professional ability, I added the graces of a manly, robust and genteel

To this latter circumstance, I think, I owe in a great measure, my renown amongst the fairer portion of my patients. My success with these, in love as well as physic, was really marvellous, and I have had as many as three or four people coming to my house in one day for medicine, not altogether of a nauseous description.

My father at this time was living at Broad Heath, his residence in the locality; there he kept a mistress, and being himself a bachelor, he spent the most of his time in her society. In my capacity as medical adviser to the family, an office which carried a key to fit all the doors, I had frequently seen and spoken to this lady; she was a woman of perhaps nearly thirty years of age, tall, slender, yet not thin, carrying in all her movements that particular grace which is only possessed by females of this stamp, far from dark, yet sufficiently inclined towards the brunette to prevent her being called fair, with large and full brown eyes, in which floated constantly the light of youthful desire, unsullied by contact with the ruining hand of public prostitution, and fresh from her native atmosphere; her manners were easy and graceful, and her conversation charming.

With this lady my fancy soon found a resting place, and full of notions of revenging Lord L—'s desertion of my mother, I allowed myself to cherish ideas of putting in practice a signal retribution.

Adelaide, that was the name of this full-blown rose, exhibited in all her intercourse with me so much condescension and regard that I had but little difficulty in persuading myself, her conquest would prove an easy victory.

I endeavoured to insinuate myself into her confidence, and hitting upon a few of her weak points, I soon found myself in a position to open the breach.

Gradually allowing my feelings to become visible, and watching the effects upon the lady, she appeared to me to be flattered by partiality and she smiled on my suit. Opportunity only was now wanted to complete the adventure, and it was not long before it occurred.

One day I was making my usual afternoon's round amongst my patients, when on passing the gates I perceived the chariot of Lord L— emerge with his lordship seated alone with it. Waiting until it had turned an angle of the road, and was well out of sight, I went up to the house, and asked for his lordship—of course he was not at home—and as I was turning, as if to depart, I suddenly asked for the lady, making an excuse about some flowers I had promised her.

Being admitted, I found her seated alone, having just parted from my father; we entered into conversation, and I studied to improve the opportune chance by every means in my power.

Not to weary the reader by detailing every passing compliment or meaning look, suffice it to say a quarter of an hour found us side by side upon a sofa, with my arm tenderly pressed round the waist of the lovely woman. From this position it was easy to snatch an occasional kiss, and finding no great resistance to this liberty, I proceeded cautiously to others still more daring.

My hand wandered over the palpitating bosom of my fair friend, and I gradually turned myself towards her, until our faces met, and my chest pressed her softer charms beneath it.

Our eyes met; there was no necessity for words, the soft voluptuous languor in her humid optics was far more expressive than words of the amorous storm within that tumultuous bosom.

Fierce lust now took full possession of me, and no consideration, however sacred, would have prevented me from gratifying my burning passion upon the person of the lovely being before me.

I sought and found the hem of her dress, and without experiencing much opposition, succeeded in passing my hand up to her knees; it did not stop there, but with redoubled ardour it aspired to take possession of things above. A thigh of large and beautifully moulded proportions ravished me with its softness, yet further, a mossy growth of fine down hair rewarded the boldness of my searching hand.

Wound up to a fearful pitch of excitement, I worked my finger into as charming a little recess as ever tempted man.

Delays are dangerous, more especially in love, so say the eager, and so thought I, as stealthily unbuttoning my nether garments, I slyly introduced my firm and excited weapon to the lovely spot. A voluptuous shudder passed through her frame the first touch. I press forward, a murmur of resentment breaks gently from the lips of my companion; I feel the commencement of the soft insertion, and bursting with impatience, I bury myself in the body of the dear girl.

Once fairly in, how I did revel in charms of such a luxurious nature. Fiercely did I move in and out of the tight, lusciously clasping case, which clung so amorously with its soft juicy folds to the shaft of my delighted weapon of love.

At each thrust she sighed more deeply, and as the maddening moments passed, and the intense enjoyment lashed our passions into fury, she hugged my form closely to her, whilst low murmurs of wanton pleasure escaped from the dewy lips which had just previously essayed to express her resentment at my outrageous conduct.

Nature could no longer restrain her tribute to the efforts of love, which now produced their usual effect, but in a more exaggerated form. I felt the approach of those moments, during which we die a thousand deaths, as the fires of fierce lightning dance through every nerve. It came; I fell forward. Description is vain to paint my feelings. A quivering agony of pleasure seized us both—a delirious desire to press our souls and bodies closer in communication, a mutual rush of that hot balm, which finally relieves excited nature, closed out transports and left us breathless, hot, and moist in each other's arms.

We remained for some moments closely entwined in each other's embrace, and exchanging those little gentle tokens of gratified passion that usually mark the period of listlessness, succeeding the fierce energy of previous action.

At length we separated, but only to adjust our somewhat ruffled habiliments. She then made me sit down by her side, and it was not long, before I found my champion growing restive beneath the touches of the soft warm hand, which she had inserted into his nest. Not contented however that he should remain thus concealed, she with a slight jerk brought my stately toy into daylight, the proceeded to examine it in every direction.

This amusement I found highly gratifying to my own senses, and soon induced such a state of erection as to give fair promise of a refreshing spurt to the lovely operator.

A new idea seemed to strike her, and sliding on to her knees between my legs, she wantonly caressed my member, all hard and excited as it was, and after lengthened hisses, slowly let it slide into her mouth, and then so tickled it with her tongue, and pressed it between her moist lips, that I was fain to cry "hold!" and abruptly withdrew my instrument for fear of a discharge. But if I deprived myself of one opportunity, I quickly found another opening, not less delightful than the less usual entrance I had just quitted.

We gave ourselves entirely up to the rage of our voluptuous sensations; I wriggled and pushed, until I lay gasping on her breast in the soft agonies of a bountiful emission.

Again and again I cooled my raging lust, in the arms of this charming woman, who was ever ready to respond with all the ardour of her sensuous nature to the continued resurrections of Cupid's battering ram, which she laughingly assured me was a perfect phoenix of its kind.

At last exhausted nature refused longer to sustain my desires, and after much loving dalliance and promises of a speedy re-union, the hig-hmettled pego had to confess himself vanquished, and slunk away crestfallen from the field of love.

CHAPTER II

When Sappho loved a fair being of her own sex even to madness, she doubtless found a means to gratify the passion with which she burned, although to us men, and more especially to medical men, it is surprising how a perfect enjoyment could be arrived at, without a penetrating power on either side.

Woman is formed to receive within her the all-important member of the other sex, and if she is deprived of that, there is but one substitute to compensate for the loss, and that is imagination. But the inspired poetess possessed imagination in an inordinate degree, and no doubt she brought it into play, in those soft encounters of which the old Greek writers tell us, a sufficient amount of that essential to constitute a pleasure no less keen than a novel.

And so in the present day what is wanting in absolute reality, is an imaginative mind supplied by the fancy. When a man gives himself up to the pleasures of self-enjoyment, does not the idea that he is procuring these agreeable sensations my unnatural means, tend to heighten his feelings. And does he not try to picture – aye, to a marvelous exactness, how he would feel, were those finishing throbs of ecstasy experienced upon the panting bosom of the lovely being he is lusting for?

Even so, this pleasure, in whatever degree it is experienced, is ever to be increased by the action of the mind. You are mounted on the body of a woman of pleasure, you imagine, perhaps in ignorance, that you are the first to pluck the maiden flower from a lovely and innocent girl. Have you not precisely the same sensations that would be experienced in the actual deflowering of a maid? Of course you have; and in no case can the adage be more properly applied, than when in allusion to such a deception it is remarked: "Where ignorance is bliss, 'tis folly to be wise."

The mind has everything to do with the action of the body in matters of this nature, as in all others, and in none in a more direct degree. It is the knowledge that you are engaged in the act of the greatest indecency, that you are in fact uniting the most outrageously sensual part of your body to that of a no less sensual part than the woman's person; that you have pushed that lascivious instrument of yours to the utmost within her belly, and that you are about to flood her very vitals with a stream of that all wondrous fluid with which man is endowed.

That is what constitutes the zest of enjoyment with a man of sensual mind, and any pictures which add additional piquancy to the act, are provocative of increased ardour and enjoyment.

I have wandered out of the course of my narrative in rather a discursive manner, but I must beg forgiveness of my readers for the foregoing homily, as it may explain in some measure the acts which are to follow, and which might otherwise appear purposeless.

With my fair friend of the preceding pages I passed the following morning. In her arms I wantoned away a couple of hours; again she gave me the same pleasure, and once more she received the strong champion of her desires between other lips than those naturally formed for it. This time I was resolved to let matters have their course.

She sucked and pressed my prick with her lips and tongue – it grew excited; still the delicious friction was continued, and new excitement added, until I was obliged to caution the fair girl of the inevitable result. She redoubled her caresses; nature could stand it no longer, and with a fierce cry of furious delight I discharged in her mouth, which was filled with the creamy proofs of my perfect enjoyment.

So far from resenting this premature result, she evidently relished the termination of the scene, and swallowed the sperm with the gusto of a determined votary of Priapus.

Since this adventure I have known many women prefer by far to have the seminal shower bestowed upon their mouths, rather than receive it in their cunts, and I have enjoyed in more than one instance the pleasures of a similar penchant.

Although my conquest pleased me at the moment, I soon found the temperament of the lady was not such as to ensure a lasting ascendency over me, and about two months after our first embraces, we were parted in a rather unexpected manner.

I had gone one day to visit Adelaide as, usual, at a time when I knew Lord L— was absent, and I was about to enter the conservatory, on my way to the drawing room, when the sound of voices in that apartment made me pause. They appeared to be those of a man and woman, and I had no difficulty in recognizing the latter as belonging to my fair friend.

Curiosity and a stronger feeling caused me to approach cautiously; as I advanced, I heard evident sounds of ardent osculation, and placing myself behind the half-opened door, I plainly saw a scene I shall never forget.

Lying on a sofa, her plump buttocks elevated upon the round end, and resting herself on her chest and elbows, with her clothes thrown over her back, disclosing all her most secret treasures, was Adelaide; while standing behind her bottom, his trousers about his legs, and his prick standing up in front of him like a constable's staff, was the six-foot butler, a tall strapping fellow of most important dimensions. As may be readily supposed, he was not long idle; making a passage between the cheeks of my little Adelaide's bottom, he plunged his tremendous prick up to the hilt in the cunt of my young lady, who by the wriggling of her buttocks, and the low murmurs of delight which I could distinctly hear, as she endearingly besought him to push and give her all he could, was evidently greatly relishing the assault of her huge antagonist.

At it they went: He all fury and lust, and she not in the least less wantonly excited.

As the huge yard moved in and out of its moist sheath, it literally glistened in the sunlight, while the beams of old Phoebus were full upon them. (What luscious sights were old Sol must often enjoy, and he deserves it too, as but for his enlivening warmth we, poor mortals, should be little fitted for the pleasures of coition). I saw the stretched lips of her delicious cunt close on his prick with such a force of suction, as I knew would soon prove their amply sufficient power to bring him to a crisis, but, alas! Infidelity, at least in this instance, was to meet fitting reward.

As the sturdy butler drove against the yielding bottom of the fair girl, the concussion caused the sofa to move forwards by slow degrees, carrying with it its lovely and wanton burden, until it reached a small table, whereon was placed a set of Chinese chessmen arranged for battle on the ivory board. As the sofa reached this table, a tremendous lunge from the now dreadfully excited fuckster overturned the obstacle with a loud crash, and my lovely but faithless Adelaide, raising her head to discover the cause of the disturbance, overbalanced the sofa, making it rear up on one end, must as the crisis of the stalwart champion approached, brought the frightened girl bodily upon him; in fact, at the very moment of the coming ecstasy of emission, when quite unprepared for such a shock, she fell back, and carried her companion to the floor as well, where he lay with her upon him in a half fainting state, as he still lightly clasped his love around her buttocks, his instrument of pleasure standing up between her open legs, and inundating her belly, neck, and even her face with a copious shower of sperm.

It was in this position that I surprised the combatants on entering the room; imagine the horror of the big butler, and the confusion of Adelaide!

Gathering up his trousers, the guilty domestic made a rapid exit, and I was left alone with the softer culprit, who, between rage and terror, could hardly contain herself. She reproached me with intruding on her privacy.

"Yes, my pet," I replied, "I am so sorry for having disturbed such a truly delightful séance of love. I owe you a thousand apologies,, my dear Adelaide; may I be allowed to atone for it by finishing what Perkins was prevented from thoroughly accomplishing?"

My satirical smile, as I said this, drove her almost beside herself with rage. She ordered me to leave the room, and continued relentless in spite of my assertion, that I loved to go in directly after another man.

"Wretched spying beast," she hissed between her clenched teeth. So turning on my heel with a cynical observation, that I thought in her case the Eastern girdle of chastity would be very useful to her lord, I left her to her own reflections, resolving in my own mind that, as my father's place was so well filled by his butler, it was no longer necessary for his son to try to compensate his fiery mistress for that which he could only administer in insufficient doses, not enough to satisfy the craving appetite of his fair protegee.

I now renewed my application to my professional studies, and succeeding in effecting several cures in cases of importance, where the remedies applied by many eminent members of the art of healing had failed.

Among my patients, some of whose cases were successfully treated, by means of a rather novel expedient, were two sisters, the daughters of a gentleman of property in the town, the particulars regarding whom are, I consider, of sufficient interest to be related in the next chapter.

CHAPTER III

It is one of the requirements of society that the feminine portion of it should wear, at least to outward gaze, the semblance of virtue, yet there is nothing in female human nature which is more difficult to adhere to.

Among the males, society tolerates vice of all kinds, which does not actually bring the perpetrator within the pale of the law; but with woman one false step, nay, the very breath of slander is sufficient to cast her, a degraded being, without the pale of its magic circle.

Can we picture a more pitiable position than that of a young woman, in the prime of her youth and beauty, condemned to await in silence the advance of the opposite sex, with the knowledge that the person whom she is prevailed upon to accept at last, may after all turn out to be an impostor, totally disqualified for performing those functions which are necessary to the happiness of married life.

We, medical men, are not ignorant of the secret pangs and unruly desires which consume the bashful virgin, and which society with its ordinances alone prevent her from finding a safe vent for. We have often the means of tracing all the passionate thoughts, and sometimes the wanton doings in secret of those whom kind society has condemned to disease, rather than to allow nature to take its own proper course, and allay those symptoms so detrimental to young girls.

Who shall say, how many victims have been sacrificed on the altar of mock modesty for fear, lest the disgrace of the only natural cure for their complaint should blast their characters.

I have alluded to the circumstances which have come to my knowledge from tine to time, with reference to the expedients made use of, to allay those raging fires which in too many cases prematurely exhaust the constitutions of our young women, and one of these cases will suffice to prove, how ingenious are the designs to cheat society of its whimsical requirements.

A young lady, not yet eighteen years of age, was under my care for a complaint of the bladder, in which the symptoms denoted the presence of calculus, or stone. An operation became necessary, which the patient underwent with unexampled fortitude.

I could not conceal a suspicion from the first that the young girl could, if she choose, enlighten us to the nature of the case, but strange to say, she absolutely preferred to submit to a painful and dangerous operation, with the knowledge that death might possibly ensue rather than render us any information which might lead to a correct conclusion.

The operation was performed successfully. A mass of calculus was removed, and as these formations never take place without something to build up a "nucleus," we began to search.

We recommended the usual examination, when we discovered that the formation had for its nucleus a hair-pin, which must have been introduced by the fair hands of the young patient herself, and doubtless not without a sufficient covering to render the insertion tolerably agreeable.

The result was that the inexperienced girl had allowed the hair-pin to become disengaged, and instead of getting into the entrance she had intended, it had slipped into the urethra, and thence into the bladder, from whence the very nature of its shape had prevented its returning.

This instance is only one of a number I could give my readers, illustrative of the shifts young ladies are frequently driven to, in order to satisfy in secret by illicit means, those desires which they are prevented from openly exhibiting, and which they dare not appease by nature's only fit and proper remedy, connection with the other sex.

I have promised in these pages a faithful recital of events, which have befallen me, have left a sufficiently warm interest in their remembrance to entitle them to a place here, and true to this promise I am about to relate my adventure in the case of the sisters before alluded to.

As I have already stated, they were daughters of an opulent resident in the town. They both inherited the pretty face and elegant form of their mother, who when they were quite children, had committed them in their last hours to their father's paternal regard.

I was the medical attendant of the family, and as such it fell to me to be depository of such little complaints as these two young beauties had to make. At the time I write, the elder was just sixteen, and her sister not yet fifteen.

I had of late observed in the older those usual indications of approaching puberty, that disturb the imagination of young girls, and I knew from her symptoms that nature was working powerfully within her to establish her claim to be treated as a woman.

One day on calling, I found that found Mr. H— had gone out hunting, and would not return until late in the evening. It was then four o'clock in the afternoon of a hot and close summer day. The two young creatures were alone, and received me with the modest grace so captivating to a young man.

I stood and chatted, until the time for paying my other visits had passed, and as none of them were pressing and could as well be paid the following day, I remained to tea.

After tea the younger of the two girls complained of headache, and after a little while she went up stairs to lie down, leaving her sister to sustain the conversation.

I played the agreeable with all my powers of attraction. I gazed on her with longing eyes. My looks followed every movement of her body, and my wandering fancy drew an exquisite picture of all her concealed beauties.

Gradually love grew into ardent desire – a desire so strong that I had some difficulty to keep my seat, while my rampant member stood beneath my trousers with the strength of a bar of iron.

Each moment only served to increase my fever, while I fancied I observed an embarrassment on her part, which seemed to hint that she was not ignorant of the storm that raged within me. Innocent as she was, and all inexperienced in the ways of the world, nature stirred within her powerfully, and doubtless whispered that there was some hidden fascination in my gaze, something wanting to content her.

At length tea-things were sent away, and I could find no reasonable excuse to linger longer by the beautiful being who had so fiercely tempted me.

I rose to go. She rose also. As she did so a certain uneasiness in her manner assured me that she had something to communicate. I asked her if she felt unwell, pretending that I observed an unusual paleness on her lovely face.

She said she had something to tell me, and proceeded to detail the usual symptoms of a first perception of the menses, &c., which had occurred a few days previously, and which had at first much alarmed her.

I re-assured her on this subject, explained the cause, and promised relief. And on taking my departure I requested her to come to my house on the following day, and said I would then investigate her case.

With what impatience I passed the interval, may be easily imagined by any of my readers who have been similarly situated. But as the longest night must have at length an end, so did this, and morning broke to dispel the restless dreams of unruly passion which had held me enthralled.

I anxiously awaited the time of my young patient's arrival, and my heart danced with joy, as I heard her timid knock at my street-door.

She entered – heavens! how my prick stood – how beautiful she looked. I stand even now when I think of that sweet vision.

Over a plain skirt of black silk she wore a mantle, such as becomes young ladies, with a neat little bonnet. Pale kid-gloves set off her exquisite little hands, and I noticed that her feet were encased in boots any lady might have envied.

I hastened to make her take a seat in my study. I entered fully into the particulars of her case. I found as expected, that she was experiencing the full force of those sensations which were never intended to be borne without relief, a relief I was panting to administer.

I told her of the cause of her own symptoms. I gradually explained their effects, and without shocking her modesty, I contrived to hint at the remedy.

I saw she trembled as I did so, and fearful of overreaching my purpose, I broke off into a warm condemnation of that state of society which allowed such complaints to blast in secret the youth and beauty of young girls like herself.

I went on to hint at the evident necessity, there was for the medical man supplying those deficiencies which society left in the education of young ladies.

15

I spoke of the honourable faith which they maintained in such cases, and of the impossibility of anything entrusted to them ever becoming known.

I saw that she was so innocent as to be ignorant of my purpose, and burning with lust I determined to take advantage of her inexperience, and to be the first to teach her that intoxicating lesson of pleasure which, like all roses, is not plucked without a thorn.

I gradually drew near her. I touched her – she trembled. I passed an arm around her slender waist, the contact literally maddened me. I proceeded to liberties which to a more experienced girl could have left no doubt of my intention.

Upon her my touches had only the effect of exciting more strongly within her breast those sensations of which she already complained.

I was now fairly borne away by my passions, and throwing my arms round the innocent beauty, I covered her face and neck with fierce humid kisses.

She appeared to be overcome by her feelings, and seizing the moment I lifted her like a child from her chair, and placed her on a couch. I removed her bonnet, and without meeting with any resistance from my victim, for contending emotion had rendered her all but senseless.

I carefully raised up her clothes. As I proceeded, I unveiled beauties enough to bring the dead to life, and losing all regard to delicacy I threw them over the bosom of the sweet girl. Oh, heavens! what a sight met my gaze, as slightly struggling to escape from my grasp she disclosed fresh secrets.

Everything now lay bare before me, her mossy recess, shaded by only the slightest silky down, presented to my view two full pouting lips of coral hue, while the rich swell of her lovely thighs served still further to inflame me.

I could gaze no longer. Hiding her face with the upturned clothes I hastily unbuttoned my trousers. Out flew my glowing prick, standing like a Carmelite's. I sank upon her body; she heaved and panted with vague terror. I brought my member close to the lips. I pushed forward, and as I did so, I opened with my trembling fingers the soft folds of her cunt. I repeated my thrusts. Oh, heavens! how shall I describe what followed.

I gained a penetration. I was completely within the body of the dear girl. I sank upon her almost fainting with delight, my prick panting and throbbing in her belly. Oh, the ineffable bliss of that encounter. My pen trembles as I revert to the scene.

What followed, I scarcely know. I pushed again and again, until I felt myself getting dangerously near the crisis.

I observed her soft and still gloved hand beside the couch, I seized it, and covered it with kisses. Heavens! what fire ran through me. I burned; I was on the point of spending.

Not unmindful of her reputation, even at that intoxicating moment I felt the approach of the blissful moment of emission, with fear I thrust once more. My prick seemed to traverse the full extent of her belly.

Then groaning in the agony of rapture, I drew out my bursting member, and falling prone upon her I drenched her little stomach and thighs with almost a supernatural flood of sperm.

I lay for some time so utterly overcome with the intensity of my feelings that I could only close my eyes and press the dear girl to my breast.

At length I rose, and carefully removing the reeking traces of victory, I adjusted the tumbled clothes of my companion, and then taking her tenderly in my arms, I placed her in an easy chair.

I shall not attempt to describe all the degrees she went through, before she came finally to herself, and to a full knowledge of her complete womanhood. That she never blamed me for the part I had acted was the best guarantee that she had not regretted the accomplishment of my pleasing conquest.

On recovering from the confusion and dismay, consequent upon the event I have just narrated, my fair patient lost none of her volubility, but talked away on the subject of our recent encounter, and asked so many questions that I had hardly time to reply to them, ere she puzzled me with fresh ones.

Before she left me I had initiated her into the exact proportions and nature of that potent invader, whose attack she had so lately sustained.

The handling to which my prick was now subjected in no way reduced its desire for a second engagement, but a consideration for the delicate state of my new made disciple, and the tender condition which I knew her very little privates must be in, induced me reluctantly to postpone any further attempt, and she departed from my house, if not a maid, yet a perfect woman.

CHAPTER IV

Nothing could exceed the caution with which we concealed our secret enjoyments from every jealous eye, and yet I trembled lest my indiscretion should become known.

There was only one thing for which we both panted, and that seemed too dangerous to be put into execution. Julia had often received the entire length of my large member in her little cunt, but that was the sum total of our bliss; to emit there was more than I dared.

Several weeks had elapsed since the commencement of our intercourse, and during that period I had been unremitting in my attentions to the youthful charms of my new acquisition.

She pined for the enjoyment, but I knew the risk of indulging her in her desires. Fear of getting her with child was with me always paramount, for although as a medical man I might have enabled her to get rid of the burden before maturity, yet I was alive to the dangers attendant on so serious an undertaking.

One day, as with many sighs and much regret on both sides, we proposed to omit the most usual way of finishing the performance for the Cyprian rites, Julia gave vent.

Julia, worked up almost to frenzy by the sweet friction, refused to permit my withdrawal and throwing her arms round my loins, she finally detained me, while with wanton heaves and every exertion in her power, she endeavoured to bring me to the spending point.

I was alarmed for safety, and vainly struggling to free my rampant prick from the warm sticking folds that environed it.

The more I struggled the closer she held me, and the more I drew to the dreaded moment the more she exerted herself to produce the feared emission.

"Stop, stop," I cried. "Julia, my darling girl, I shall do it, I know I shall. Oh!"

I could say no more, but with a violent drive forward I sank spending on her belly; my prick fairly buried in her up to the hair, and the semen spouting from me in torrents.

As for my wanton companion she threw back her head, and received the dangerous fluid with as much enjoyment as if it were herself who was trembling in the rapturous agony of its emission.

Trembling in every limb, as much from the fear of the result as from the excitement of the act, I rose and helped the tender Julia to her feet.

As she got up, a heavy pattering sound announced the return of the fluid which fell in large drops upon the carpet, and ran in rills down her beautiful thighs.

A few days after this affair we were diverting ourselves with sundry little freedoms one towards the other, when Julia seizing my prick in her soft white little hand, threw herself upon the sofa, and drawing me to her, commenced to kiss and toy with my member. This, as may be supposed, afforded me considerable pleasure, and I let her do what she pleased, wondering all the time what her next gambol would be.

From kissing she took to sucking, and this delicious touch of drawing lips soon inflamed me beyond all restraint.

Again she took it from between her lips, and holding the loose skin tightly in her grasp, she made her hand pass rapidly up and down the huge white shaft until I heated to the utmost and almost spending, I jerked it out of her grasp.

"Ah, my lad, you were afraid it would come out, were you?"

I replied that I was only just in time to prevent it, upon which with a laugh and a smack on the ticklish part in question, she exclaimed: "Well, then, my fine fellow, we shall see what we can make come out of that large round head of yours."

Then suiting the action to the word she again commenced the agreeable titillation, until with nerves strained to the utmost pitch of luxurious excitement, I felt the approach of that rapturous ejaculation.

Jutting out my member before me I heaved my buttocks up and down, and with a few motions of her hand Julia fairly brought me to the emitting point.

With a sigh of heavenly enjoyment I let fly the hot gushes of sperm on her bosom, while her fair hand retaining hold of my throbbing prick, received a copious flood upon its dainty surface.

After this we would frequently lie down together on the soft hearthrug, and each with a caressing hand on prick and cunt, produce in one another those delightful effects which, say what people will, give a spur to the passions no man or woman can resist.

We would operate on one another in this way until prudence compelled us to stop for fear of the concluding overflow, and then waiting for a few minutes, would once more bring our senses to the verge of the impending flood. These hours were wiled away until a serious cause of anxiety arose to put an end to our security.

As I had feared, Julia proved with child; how could she be otherwise, with such an opportunity.

As soon as she made me acquainted with the fact, I prescribed for her but without effect. The prolific juice had taken firm hold, and nature was progressing in the formation of the little squalling consequences of our amour.

My anxiety was now intense least the discovery I saw impending should, in spite of our endeavours, overwhelm us.

Under these circumstances I determined to take a resolute course. I operated on my little Julia. I succeeded. I brought away the foetus, and removed with it all danger of discovery.

The result was not so favourable with regard to the health of my patient. Our overheated passions had put an end to youth's dream of uninterrupted enjoyment in a continual round of sensual pleasure, and Julia had now to reap the harvest of her indiscretion. She soon fell into a weak state of health, and I recommended immediate change of air.

Her father, alarmed at her indisposition, took her to Baden, and after a residence of some months there, the roses again revisited her cheeks.

At Baden, she was greatly admired, and soon received an offer for her hand, which her prudent father did not feel justified in refusing and she became the wife of a Russian prince, who if he did not get with her that unsatisfactory jewel, her maidenhead, at least became possessed of a cunt well practised in all the arts of love and lechery.

Thus terminated my amour with one of the most agreeable and most salacious girls I have ever known, and my prick still stands at the recollection of the various luscious scenes in which we have mutually carried away by the violence of lust in its most enticing form.

CHAPTER V

I now gave myself up without reserve to the pleasure of love. All my patients who showed the least susceptibility were overcome by my potent argument, and vigorously fucked.

I varied my pleasures in every possible way. Nothing which could enhance the enjoyment did I scruple to call into action. I fucked. I kissed. I sucked. I underwent all these operations myself, and I found a delicious retreat between the buttocks of one of my fairest patients, I hesitate not to own it. I penetrated those regions intended by nature for further purposes, and I declare that the pleasure I derived was proportionally as great as the act itself was indecent.

I became a lover of this mode of dalliance and never spent with so much relish and impetuosity as in the beautiful bottom of a fair woman.

And it must be owned that these parts themselves are wonderfully well adapted for the purpose. The natural construction of the entrance, the soft interior, and the length with which they are capable of receiving the longest male member, render the art unique; while the fiery heat experienced by the operator, and the accumulation of delicious sensations, produce in their turn a stiffness, a vigour, and enjoyment without parallel.

One of our greatest poets, he whom no censure, no authority could debase to mere conventualism, extols in his own fervent gloomy strains the much forbidden pleasure:

Oh, lovely woman, by your maker's hand
For man's delight and solace wisely planned;
Thankless is she whose nature's bounty mocks,
Nor gives love entrance wheresoe'er he knocks.

A considerable portion of my pleasure consisted in reading and showing to others curious amorous works. Of these I possessed a large collection. Several of them were in themselves a budget of exciting literature, of a rare and costly description.

One of them was the celebrated work of the Marquis de Sade, over which it is said that extraordinary man went out of his mind.

I allude to "Justine," and if the quintessence of sexual excitement and glowing scenes that beggar description can be productive of sufficient effect to produce such a result, even to the author himself, this rare and fearful work is certainly the one capable of doing so. The wonderful descriptions it contains, the fiercely exciting scenes it depicts, and the exhibition of so many varied means of producing the acme of enjoyment, render it no less valuable for its deep effectual influence over the passions than for its deep philosophy and wonderful power of reasoning which stamp it as the work of a genius of extraordinary talent.

Satiety, that enemy to the indulgence of the soft enjoyment, now attacked me, I wanted a change. My powers were naturally great, my health robust. My member became sick of sliding in and out of places so often visited, and in which it had so frequently left his tears of gratitude.

I longed for an unripe beauty, a young girl, a child even – to caress, to lie with, to suck. I found a lovely little girl of thirteen years of age, who had been under my care for a spinal affliction, in the treatment of which complaint I had been for a long time acknowledged a successful practitioner.

She had been an inmate of my house in order to be more fully under my care. Her friends were resident in another county, and had such confidence in my discretion that I believe had I even proposed to have slept with their niece they would have thought it was only a part of my system.

Mary had been with me about a week, when I found so much pleasure in her society that I began to feel a curious sensation about the region of my privates on beholding and listening to her sometimes in the evening.

I made her sometimes sit with me by the fire, when I would place her on my knee, so that her sweet little bottom would be immediately over my stiffened member, which by its throbbing and jerks caused her to sit rather uneasily, and thereby induced a gentle friction which was highly agreeable to me.

One evening, having been more than a week without food for my passions, which were becoming riotous, I could restrain myself no longer. I began to play and romp with my little companion in such a manner that I frequently had my hand on her naked knee, and even once or twice on her thigh.

Her flesh felt soft and warm, and my desires began to master my reason. I tried further advances, taking care not to startle the innocent girl out of her confidence in me.

By degrees, under the pretence of tickling her to excite her laughter, I reached the goal of my desires. My hand, the tip of my fingers only, touched her pouting little beardless cunt. A thrill shot through at the contact. It was soft as her damask cheek, and the warmth of its velvet skin sent fire through my veins.

I now endeavoured to advance, but she held her legs firmly together, not apparently altogether relishing the tickling sensation my intrusion produced.

She was an excitable little girl, however, and soon, by suddenly pretending to throw her backwards, I got her to open her legs. And then, oh! how I stand when I even refer to it. I placed my smooth fingers in the open slit; it was as moist as the interior of her lovely mouth, and the opening was small, and apparently intact.

My readers may wonder perhaps at the above remark, but my experience has shown me that in very many cases young girls, long before they reach the age of fourteen, cannot strictly be said to be possessed of a perfect maidenhead.

The cause is this. What with the early efforts prompted by nature to break through the restraints she has herself placed in that tender spot, by the self-introduction of their little fingers, and other inanimate objects, and the effects of the society, and even the bed-fellowship of boys from twelve to fourteen years of age, who frequently effect a penetration in very young children with their small but stiffly erected member, young girls on reaching puberty are seldom possessed of the imaginary jewel in its full perfection, at least so far as regards the lower and middle classes of society.

I could enumerate many instances of the truth of what I here affirm. For instance, I recollect a case which occurred at school at which my father had placed me.

The master of the academy had a little daughter, nearly twelve years of age, when the circumstance happened to which I am now drawing attention. This child was allowed considerable liberty, and she would after school hours mingle with us in the playground.

There were not wanting boys ready to take advantage of such opportunity to investigate the hidden treasures of nature. Little Miss being inspired with a similar desire, soon had several admirers, with whom it was a delightful pastime to feel and tickle each other's curious little secrets.

From feeling they soon arrived at conjunction, and it was not many days before one of the boys possessed of a longer and stiffer instrument than his companions, fairly penetrated her gentle belly, and deposited his little drops of pleasure within her vagina.

He was of course followed by others, and this young girl, before she reached the age of twelve and who was considered by her parents an emblem of innocence, became the juvenile harlot of the school of thirty boys, and rarely passed a day without receiving the vigorous attacks of at least three or four of them.

A discovery came at last, but not before a junior usher, a tall, strong, young fellow of twenty had himself found out the state of matters, and under a threat of disclosing the affair had forced the little girl to submit to his own embraces.

In consequence of this unusual attack, and the pain she suffered from the distention of her parts by the much greater size of the new champion, the doctor discovered the affair, and they removed the child at once.

But to return to myself and my little playmate.

When she found my hand in possession of what she had no idea of the use of, she tried all in her power to disengage herself, but I took care her struggles should be unavailing, and at length she laughingly ceased them.

I now roamed over her little charms at pleasure, but my prick was up, my boiling point was reached, and I cautiously laid her lengthwise on the sofa, and getting on her pulled out my member standing stiff.

Moistening it well with saliva I put it to the tender orifice and pushed. Up to this time my young companion had no idea of my intention, and wonderingly submitted to my caresses. She now felt the painful pressure I was causing with the large had of my prick, and would have averted my attack but that I kept her steady with my left arm round her waist.

Again and again, I attempted the entrance. I was foiled, until suddenly a squirt of sperm came to my assistance. Once more trying the now moistened barrier, the head of my prick went gradually in as far as its junction with the shaft. There it stuck, and my excitement being now at its height, I spent. The hot thick fluid escaped from me in streams, and inundated the soft and stretched interior of her belly.

During the emission I gained about another inch, but no more, and only at the expense of much pain to my youthful mistress.

In the course of the following day I repeated my attempts upon Mary's little fortress, and at length demolished her natural defences, and plundered the whole length of my machine into her vagina. The enjoyment was extreme, and the tightness of her little unshaded cunt soon brought on a most plentiful shower of semen, which I freely poured into her, secure by reason of her tender age from any unpleasant consequences of the amour.*

[note by the editor. The narrator was fortunate in this respect, for the confidence he expresses is certainly without foundation, as at the moment of going to press with this work, he knows of a case, the little daughter of a stevedore at Bermondsey, who, although not eleven years of age, is eight months gone in pregnancy, and when the parents first discovered the state their child was in, she had been carrying on her amour with a full-grown man for upwards of four months.]

Little Mary, when her passion had once been thoroughly aroused, proved to be most lasciviously inclined. For fear of injuring her back or putting a dangers strain upon her tender spine, I made her lie as still as possible, in which position she was delightful for me to stir up her vitals by the gentle movements of my big prick, which would quickly come to the crisis of emission, so deliciously tight did her little cunt cling round its ruby head.

She was one of the most apt little pupils I ever had in the art of gamahuching. We used to do the double, both of us stripped perfectly naked on her bed, (this was only done when I visited her in her room, after my household had all retired for the night), then she would reverse her position, and lie over me, burying my face between her thighs, whilst I returned the attentions she so delightfully bestowed on my prick, by sucking and tongue-fucking both her pink little cunt and her rosy wrinkled little bottomhole, until she spent over and over again in my mouth, each pearly drop as precious to me as the most veritable elixir of life, for streams of sperm literally spouted from my prick in response to these proofs of her ardent enjoyment. How she sucked my prick first, and then cuddled it between her throbbing titties, till it came again. What transports of ecstasy seemed to carry us both away it is impossible to describe in these pages.

She told me that she longed to feel me move within her, with all the furious energy of which she knew I was so capable, and that her having to keep still, and my gentle movements when I fucked her, only seemed to excite without giving her that full satisfaction which she instinctively felt could only be obtained by giving full license to all our desires by a perfect abandon of voluptuousness in those ecstatic conjunctions of which I had hitherto so imperfectly given her an idea, of the heavenly joys she yet anticipated to receive in my arms, adding that she had most enjoyed it, when I completed her ravishment on the second day of my attempt, and that although she had actually fainted under the excruciating pain caused by the entrance of my big affair into her tight little cunny, yet in her trancelike swoon she had experienced such supernatural pleasure, as she had never felt since.

"Do, darling," she added, "fuck me with real energy, if only for once; do let me feel what the ecstasies of sexual conjunction are really like; let me die of love for once, if I am never able to bear it again. You know the complaint, my spinal affliction, will never let me recover sufficiently to be married."

Thus appealed to by the loving little Mary, I consented to fuck her properly, but only on one condition, and that was that she must allow me to tie her down, face downward over the couch in my surgery, so that I might give her every possible satisfaction by my own movements, and yet be sure that she would not injure herself by twisting about as I know that otherwise in the abandon of her ecstasy she would be almost certain to do.

The next afternoon, just as I was certain all the morning calls were over, and was looking over my notes to see what visits I had to pay, a gentle tap at the surgery-door reminded me of my promise to Mary.

She entered, saying with a most bewitching smile on her usually pensive face: "Now, sir, I mean to keep you to your word; do you think I will let you go round and fuck half a dozen of your lady patients first, why there would be nothing left for poor little Polly. I want every drop of that life-giving fluid; if I die, you shall be as dry as a stone before you go out today."

My time was really precious, but there was no gainsaying the darling, so with many preliminary kisses and endearing touches, I first locked the door. Then we both divested ourselves of everything we had on. My impediments were only dressing-gown and trousers, whilst Mary was also in equally light marching order.

The couch I proposed to lay her down upon was a veritable battleground of Venus, having been made for my special use, according to ideas which I furnished to my upholsterer; and could my readers but have the experience of that sofa, instead of this partial scrawl, they would indeed have a repletion of luscious adventures, ad nauseam.

To return to my tale, this couch was very wide, with no back, and a scroll-head at one end, whilst what would be considered the foot was half-moon shaped, so that when a bottom or a pretty cunt was exposed to my attack, I could stand well between the open legs of my fair patient and administer my natural clyster with the greatest possible east to myself, either standing or kneeling on a hassock.

This couch had a most beautiful springy motion when under a pair of lively lovers, being constructed with a special eye to luxurious effect, and it had also screws at each end and in the centre, so that I could elevate the head, bottoms, or bodies of my patients to suit the ideas to be carried out.

Mary was all docility, and quietly placed herself on her belly upon this throne of love; using cords to secure her by the wrists and ankles, I then finished the tying by firmly fastening her body down by means of a long sash passed under the sofa, and over her back.

"Now, my darling, you are completely at my mercy!" I exclaimed with a laugh. "I think I ought to birch* that naughty little bottom for you, but instead of that I will kiss it."

[I used this couch sometimes to tie down and flagellate several of my old male patients, whose early excesses had made them too used up for the sport of love, and could only enjoy the pleasures of emission under the stimulating effects of the rod. It was one of the most lucrative branches of my profession.]

Kneeling down I adjusted the height of her delicious little cunt, till it was exactly opposite my eager lips, so was also that ravishing little wrinkled orifice which nature placed so close to it, that it is impossible not to believe it ought to have its due share of attention from both prick and mouth.

She was already spending in anticipation. My tongue revelled in that creamy emission, till she was almost beside herself, and actually screamed for me to let her have my prick.

"Oh! oh! darling, I must have the real thing at once. Oh, don't tantalize me so, dearest!"

But that was not my intention at the moment. I wanted an even more luscious enjoyment, to take her second maidenhead in fact. Leaving her delicious little cunt, my tongue titillated that other rosy aperture, till she was almost mad, and her appeals for satisfaction were getting quite piteous.

"May I go in here then, darling?" I asked.

"You will find that it surpasses anything you can imagine, love."

"Yes, oh, yes, anywhere; kill me, if you like, but make me feel that ineffable pleasure which I know only a prick can give, you drive me wild!"

Cold cream was handy on the table, so well lubricating the entrance, as well as the head of my pego, my rather big prick effected an entrance much more easily than it had the first time I tried to ravish her cunt. Her face was turned round towards me, and I could see tears of pain start to her eyes, as I gradually pushed past the sphincter muscle, but then easing for a moment or two, I began slowly to move within the delicious sheath, which held my affair so tightly clasped within its folds, and throbbed so convulsively upon my delighted instrument that I could not refrain from spending, making her actually scream with delight as the warm balsam of love seemed to penetrate her very vitals.

"'How I burn, how deliciously warm, and it makes me spend more than ever. Oh! oh! frig me in front, dearest, don't let us lose an atom of such heavenly pleasure!"

It would weary my readers too much to repeat all our loving exclamations during this long and ecstatic bottom-fuck, but I will merely say that at the end of about half-an-hour, and after I had spent at least six times without withdrawing, we both actually fainted from excess of emotion, which finished our fun for that day, but it is needless to say that the performance was afterwards repeatedly given by special request of my little loving Mary.

In conclusion I may say that if the last incident appears in any way incredible, or if my reader wishes himself to taste of this fresh source of excitement, a line to the author, under cover to the agent from whom this work was procured, will enable him to convince himself by means of practical proof beyond the power of the most incredulous to doubt.

Another extraordinary thing I ought to mention, is that the fucking, &c., had such a salubrious effect upon my young patient that she eventually quite got the better of her spinal complaint, and was married at the age of eighteen, but although apparently well and strong, she never had any children.

CHAPTER VI

A curious incident befell me soon after losing Mary. I had been very virtuous for a week or two, in order to recover my usual vigour after the unreasonable requirements which my late patient had exacted from me, before she left the shelter of my roof. John Thomas was quite resuscitated by his rest, and I was already casting my eyes around for fresh food for my convent (being a strict bachelor with only an old housekeeper and a very ugly middle-aged woman as servant), when one evening in early spring, a little after dark, I was sitting in my easy chair in the surgery, in a state of reverie, my brain revolving all the luscious scenes of my experience, my prick at the moment actually at full cock, and almost ready to go off itself as I thought of how I had tied Mary down on my couch and ravished her second maidenhead.

A desperate ring at the little bell and a heavy rat-a-tat-tat on the small knocker, made me almost jump from my seat. The room was in darkness, but I opened the door quickly, when a female figure rushed in, and stumbling against the mystical sofa, sank upon it sobbing, as if her heart would break. "I'm undone, oh! oh! oh!!! doctor; what shall I do, I can't go home!"

My first idea was to light my lamp, then drawing the bolt, I approached the weeping person on the sofa, who I saw at once had been roughly handled, as her dress was torn and patched with dirt in places.

"Come, tell me what it is; who are you, let me see your face. Surely you can trust your doctor if no one else, you are not killed, and apparently only a bit troubled about something, allow me."

Saying this I raised her face to see who it was.

"Goodness gracious, it is you, Miss Lover? Now tell me all; you can confide in me sooner than your own papa, for I know the rector is very straight-laced!"

It was indeed our clergyman's only daughter, a sweet young lady of about twenty whom I had always considered quite beyond the pale of my operations, and a paragon of purity itself.

"I'm undone," she sobbed. "Oh, dear doctor, what shall I do?" she said again as she wrung her hands, and floods of briny tears coursed down her crimson cheeks.

At last I calmed her a little, and gave her a drop of cordial; then she began to tell me, sobbing all the while, how that no one knew she was secretly engaged to young Pomeroy, the squire's son, because his father would never sanction his son's marrying without money, and you know, doctor, my poor pa has only his living to depend upon, although he is so proud and thinks anyone in holy orders quite equal to the highest in the land. Well, this evening I met George in the lane at the back of your house, and he persuaded me to sit down in the little coppice in your paddock, so as to be out of hearing of anyone going down the lane. He wanted me to elope with him, and at last when every argument failed to persuade me, said he would have me then, if he was hanged for it; how I have struggled you may see, but at last I fainted from mere exhaustion, and only came to myself to find I had been ruined, and that he had left me. (I suppose he thought I was dead)." She still went on sobbing about his brutality, and the ruin he had brought upon her.

At last I persuaded her to allow me to make an examination, and found that he really had effected his purpose, the hymen being broken and bleeding, and her thighs stained with bloody semen.

"Let me advise you, my dear young lady," I said, rising from the interesting investigation which you may be sure renewed my previous cockstand, "let me advise you to go home as quietly as possible; I will call my housekeeper who is discretion itself, she will put you right, so that no one will notice anything unusual, then you shall have a lotion to soothe the lacerated parts, and come again and see me about 5 o'clock tomorrow afternoon. I will do even better than your father for you, and perhaps can see George and make him do what is proper, but take my advice, it is no use crying over spilt milk, and time and patience will bring all right in the end. At any rate I will promise to shield you from any ill effects of his brutality that might otherwise bring you to shame and disgrace."

She left protesting her everlasting gratitude for all my kindness, and begged me if possible to see George in the morning. I tried to do so, but found he had not been home all night, and had evidently absconded, as he thought he had killed Miss Lover.

I awaited her coming at 5 o'clock in a state of excited expectation, and as I nervously walked about my little surgery, kept fumbling a very mysterious something in my pocket (not my prick, but my readers may find out what it was bye and bye), which would impart a magic influence to my fingers, so that when I repeated my examination, and handled the lips of her cunt, her clitoris, &c., the effect would be so exciting that she would be ready to let me do anything to soothe her at once.

She arrived within a few minutes of the appointed time. How she blushed as I shook her hand, and told her she looked as beautiful as an angel, that I would do everything in my power to shield her from harm or disgrace.

"Now, take off your hat, and allow me to inspect the damage again, my dear young lady," I said, making her take a seat upon the couch.

"It's so delicate, but I suppose I must. Besides you know all, and will keep my secret, won't you, doctor?" she said in a low voice, crimsoning again to the roots of her hair.

"Certainly, have no fear of that, but you must remove your skirt, my dear young lady, or I cannot do what is necessary in your delicate case."

She reluctantly complied, then I made her lie backwards on the couch, and open her legs as wide as possible, as at the same time I screwed up the lower end of the sofa. Then proceeding with my examination, I fingered both clitoris, lips of the vagina, and passed them quite up into her deliciously tight cunt which was ornamented with a profusion of silky dark brown hair, between which could be seen a pair of vermilion lips, pouting as if ready to be kissed or parted by a roving prick.

My touches were magical, the vagina spasmodically contracted on my fingers, and I could see she could scarcely restrain her feelings.

"My dear Miss Lover, I'm afraid you may have a baby after such an outrage," I said, "and the only remedy I can suggest is that another man should do the same to you at once, for one will then undo any mischief left behind by the other."

"Doctor, Doctor, how awful!' she sobbed. "I would rather poison myself to hide my shame, it is impossible."

"Not quite so hopeless as you may think, my dear young lady; this is the antidote, it you will let me insert it in your lovely body," at the same instant bringing the head of my prick to the lips of that lovely cunt of hers. Her position had prevented her from seeing what I was about to do.

This touch seemed electrical, she gave a deep sigh, and then I was soon buried to the hilt in what I once more thought the most delightful grotto of love I had ever yet entered, (but almost every fresh cunt is the same at first), so warm, so tight, such lascivious pressures on my prick, that I kept still for some minutes to enjoy that sense of possession which is so sweet, when you first feel really sure that you are actually in a cunt you have been longing for. When I began to move, it at once stirred up all the hitherto latent fires of an unusually warm temperament. What mutual transports we enjoyed, swimming in a perfect sea of lubricity, she could never have enough, and I was fairly drained, when at last she released me from her arms, and shed tears of remorse over her new-found joy, which she told me she knew was so wicked to indulge in.

My readers may be sure my natural flow of eloquence did not desert me at such a crisis, and I can assure them that I made a thorough convert of this virtuous and highly religious young lady, who carried one of the sweetest liaisons of my life for three years, till old Squire Pomeroy died, and his son George came back and married the rector's daughter.

In the foregoing incident I mentioned about fumbling something in my pocket, as I walked about the room, and to enlighten my readers as to what that mysterious article was, will relate a little incident which had then only recently occurred to me.

We had a wealthy horse-dealer named Parker in our village, whose son John got married to one of the prettiest girls in the place; well, a few days after the wedding poor John, a regular country-bumpkin, came to me one morning in sad trouble: "What be I to do now, doctor, my wife Carry don't go to horse at all, zur?"

These were his exact words, as he stood despondently wiping his forehead with a red cotton handkerchief.

I had often cured John of little venereal evils, especially after he had been to London on business. As he was a rare fellow to spend his money on the girls, so I could not help fairly laughing at his question.

However, he was serious, and informed me that Carry certainly had suffered him to take her maidenhead, but that there was no pleasure in it then or since, like he had had with common women, and in fact his wife was as cold as ice, merely consenting to let him do it, because he was her husband.

I thought the case over for a minute or two, and then told him I thought that if I made an examination I might slyly apply something to make her randy and ready enough to take his prick in future.

"I'm good for a tenner, zur, if you can just make her to go horse, a bit, the stallion's up to his work, I know," saying which he took his leave, promising to send her to me in the afternoon.

The fact of his being a horse-dealer had given me an idea about ginger, and also made my cock stand so that I was glad to see him go, for fear he should observe it, and refuse to give me the chance of making him a cuckold.

Carry had always been a prude, so that when she called in the afternoon, I was almost at a loss, how to open the business.

After saying how pleased I was to see her, how well she looked, &c., I went on: "You must not mind me speaking to you, dear Mrs. Parker, seriously upon a subject, which is of the greatest possible consequence to the future happiness of both yourself and husband. In fact, he has seen me upon the subject of your being so cold and unsympathetic in the act of love, the act of coition, I ought rather to say, which unless enjoyed and fully entered into by both male and female, causes so many separations, divorces, &c. Besides you would have no children. How would you like John to go after other girls, because he has no pleasure with you? It is such a serious business, that you ought to let me make an examination, as I hope to be able to make both of you grateful to me for the rest of your lives."

After all sorts of objections and difficulties she at last seated herself on the throne of bliss, as I called it (my sofa), and allowed me to raise her clothes. I did everything with the greatest possible delicacy, telling her she had better cover up her eyes, &c. Then I examined most minutely one of the most delicious little cunts, I had ever looked into, a beautiful pinky little slit, shaded by the softest brown hair, with a delightful little pink orifice beneath it. That was where my gingered fingers first touched her, then they slowly opened the luscious lips of her love-gap, squeezed the clitoris, and gently rubbed a little inside, till I perceived very evident sighs of rapidly increasing excitement. You may be sure my cock was ready enough, so I gently introduced him to Venus' wrinkle, and John's big tosser had so effectually opened her, that I had no great difficulty in slipping in, as she was already spending and almost unconscious from excess of emotion. I spent too almost directly, (in fact, I afterwards found I really made her first baby), and then throwing my arms around her, I glued my lips to hers as I pushed on, and asked if she did not like it now.

"Could you, my darling, now refuse such bliss?" I exclaimed, as I spent for a second time. "You will go home and enjoy it with your husband in future, won't you?"

She kissed me in her frantic state of lubricity, and shed tears of sorrow to think she was not my wife, instead of John's, but as this was out of the question, she made the best of a bad job and called in my professional assistance upon every possible occasion, telling me to charge for it well in my bill, as John really owed me so much for teaching her the real joys of fucking.

Next morning her husband burst into my surgery. "Hi, Hi! Ha, Ha!! Doctor, yer made her go to horse rights now, thars her tenner, and that's only a quid of time. Ten times, zur help me God, she helped herself, when I couldn't quite come to time. When yer want a good fuck, try ginger-boys, she told me, what yer put on her, what a fool not to think of 'it myself. But it's the best I ever had for my rhino, Lunnon, or anywheres!"

It is really surprising, how many married women actually pass through life without ever feeling the real pleasure of coition. I consider that medical advisers ought to catechise young married ladies on the subject, and that it is their duty to enlighten the fair but cold innocents to the joys they lose, by simply submitting to the marriage-rites as a necessity, and not entering into the spirit of the fun.

In the foregoing pages I have endeavoured to give my readers a brief outline of my intrigues and adventures as far as they could be entered upon in so limited a space and I can only say, that if they enjoyed as many opportunities on their wanderings as have fallen to my share, they ought to have as lively a recollection of them as myself, for pleasure, though the actual indulgence of it vanishes, yet leaves the recollection ever vivid in the minds of those who have partaken of her sweet and luscious cup.

END

A NOVICE'S TEMPTATION

Anonymous

1890

A NOVICE'S TEMPTATION

"Not far from the Varennes, on the banks of the Aire," the blonde began in a dreamy way, "stands a convent, in a little valley nestling among the mountains.

"The good nuns there spend their lives in prayer and in sewing for the orphans of the village. Their number, when the convent is full, is about forty. The little church, situated in the middle of the village, counts among its flock the inhabitants of the country for ten miles round and includes the convent in question.

"The officiating priest being old and feeble, was assisted by a young Abbe who had arrived only a few days previous to the opening of this story. The young Abbe was of such modest demeanour, that even the oldest bigots of the parish took him for a saint in swaddling clothes.

"The young girls all remarked that he was undeniably handsome and when they went to the confessional, each one went early to be sure to get a chance to confess during the day.

"The old curate was not sorry to be relieved of his arduous work and it was only right that the poor man should have some rest. He now only confessed the nuns at the convent every fortnight, when they sent their old coach for him.

"It was always a treat at the convent when the venerable priest visited them. They dined in the great refectory and he seemed to bring with him an odour of out-of-doors, which always touched the hearts of the novices, who sighed every now and then under its influence.

"One day, however, the old vehicle brought the young Abbe to the convent. The old curate was ill and had sent his excuses to the Lady Superior. The latter received the young man in the parlour on the ground floor and was quite charmed with his modest bearing. They conversed at first about the curate, then about the crops, then the church. They had been repairing the chapel of St. Anthony, etc.

"The Lady Superior finally assembled the nuns in order to present them to their new pastor, and one after another they passed before him and curtsied without raising their eyes to his face. Why should they, since he was only to speak words of peace and comfort to them from behind the wooden grating.

"Three novices were the last to enter. One of them had examined the young Abbe through a crack in the door before coming in, and her cheeks became crimson as she curtsied to him.

"After the presentation the Lady Superior made a little speech and then accompanied the Abbe to the chapel, followed by the whole party of nuns.

"The young priest opened the centre door and closed it carefully after him a moment later. A slight rustling told his auditors that he was slipping on a white surplice that was hanging inside the door, then came the noise of a stool sliding across the floor, and all was silent.

"The nuns were all present except those occupied with the household duties. They had glided into the chapel more like shadows than like human beings. Two of them knelt in the confessional.

"Presently the sound of a deep voice, followed by soft whisperings was heard. The murmur ceased, then commenced again. Then came a long silence. The arms of the sinner moved restlessly as she pronounced mea culpa. The Lady Superior rose with a bowed head, her arms crossed on her breast, moved towards the little chapel of the Holy Virgin.

"All the nuns in turn came and knelt on either side of the confessional.

Finally it was the turn of the youngest novice.

"Trembling with fear and yet impatient to hear the Abbe's voice on the other side of the grating, she knelt down on her little wooden stool. By closing her eyes and stopping her ears she tried to examine her conscience. The image of the Abbe, however, would rise up before her.

She waited until the rattle of the little window warned her that he was ready to listen to her, and the confession began!

"'Your blessing, my father,' etc., etc., until the solemn moment arrived when her most secret thoughts must be unveiled.

"'My child, have you sinned in thought; have you longed for the world and the pleasures thereof?'

"She gave no answer.

"Then the Abbe whispered low: 'Have you ever had any bad thoughts? Did you ever commit any sinful deeds?'

"Still she could not answer.

"'Have you listened to the demon tempting you to sensual actions? Speak without fear, my child, God is good and will forgive.'

"'My father,' stammered the poor little novice, not understanding and yet trying to see the priest who was plying her with these terrible questions.

"She could only distinguish, however, through the grating, two flashing eyes which stirred her very soul with a magnetic influence, which the poor little novice would have been unable to define.

"'Yes, father!' she replied at last, forced to say something.

"'Have you sinned in thoughts and deeds, my child. How many times?' he then inquired, his voice trembling slightly. 'Did you commit these sins alone or have you a companion in sin? Speak, my child, to obtain pardon, you must confess all, as you can only obtain peace after a full confession. Have you given yourself up to Satan by day or by night? Be careful not to commit sacrilege. I shall be obliged to refuse you absolution the next time if you do. Meanwhile examine your conscience carefully. Pray for help. Then you can approach the communion table. Pray every night with a contrite heart. Go, my child!'

"With an unsteady step she left the chapel. That night the young nun, Sister Clemence by name, could not sleep. She tossed restlessly on her narrow bed, and could think of nothing but the words the Abbe had spoken.

"'Sinned in thoughts – yes, often I have longed to leave the convent and enter the beautiful shops in the city. Then there was Mr. Ernest, who used to come to my aunt's house. I have often thought how delightful it would be to ramble through the woods with him alone. But are these bad thoughts – sensual thoughts?' she said.

"She finally closed her eyes and fell asleep and saw Satan! Yes, it was Satan. All at once, however, he assumed the form of the Abbe.

"He took her hand and placed it between her legs. Oh, what a delicious sensation, how delightful. 'Mr. Satan, Mr. Abbe, please, please go on... don't stop... ah, this is delicious!... oh!... Mr. Abbe!!'

"Sister Clemence awoke suddenly, trembling like a leaf, weak and tired. She felt numb between her legs. Placing her hand there, she found it was wet... poor little novice, she could not understand.

"Daylight appeared at last, but Sister Clemence was unable to rest. She threw back the coverings and raised her long white chemise. She wanted to see, but there was nothing but the little stain of blood which surprised her very much at this particular time of month.

"When the great bell gave the signal for rising, Sister Clemence, usually so quick and lively, crept out of bed with difficulty and dressed herself slowly. She was the last to enter the chapel and kneeling down, joined her hands mechanically for the morning prayer.

"In the refectory she was unable to eat. When the Lady Superior arrived she questioned her. She was a sort of physician but she perceived nothing extraordinary in the symptoms of her subordinate and advised a few days of rest.

"During the eight days that Sister Clemence remained in her cell, she did not seem to improve; on the contrary, she grew worse and worse. She could not sleep and if she happened to fall into a feverish slumber, the same vision pursued her, accompanied by the same temptations. It sometimes happened that even half awake, her hands would seek the mysterious spot, centre of such delightful sensations, and unconsciously her fingers lingered there.

"Finally, entirely awake, the same irresistible power drew her fingers to the same place, but then it required a longer time to reach the point of supreme enjoyment.

"At first the novice's thoughts were not fixed upon any particular object. Then she thought of Mr. Ernest, and lastly of the Abbe. What a sacrilege!

"If you had seen this little childish hand buried between those white thighs, smooth and firm as marble, her lovely eyes partly closed and those ripe red lips slightly parted, you would have seen her body motionless at first, become slightly agitated, then the legs move further and further apart, the little finger slip in and out of the rosy mouth, until with a deep sigh, she sank back, powerless to move hand or foot.

"Two weeks had elapsed and the Abbe returned to confess the nuns. The Lady Superior called on the invalid and asked her if she wished to confess. She even said that the Abbe had kindly offered to come to her cell as she was not able to rise. How to thank the Abbe for such a favour!

"'Certainly, Mother, I should like to confess,' dutifully replied Sister Clemence.

"The Lady Superior left the cell and soon returned with the Abbe who entered with that bearing of humility he habitually assumed. He appeared most concerned at the illness of the novice and insisted that a full confession was the best possible remedy.

"Sister Clemence did not dare look at him, she was so confused. The Lady Superior retired, and the Abbe took a chair by the side of the bed.

"'Have you examined your sinful heart, my child; are you ready to make a full confession?'

"'Yes, my father!'

"The confession began. The poor little Sister did not know how to reveal what had happened. The fear, however, of not receiving absolution and communion gave her courage. She disclosed everything.

"The Abbe drew closer and closer, until she felt his breath upon her face. Her eyes were closed.

"Suddenly she felt his lips pressing hers in a long kiss. Unconsciously, a timid little kiss from her lips answered his. Then she felt a warm hand upon her body, which gradually seemed to move downward towards that spot where Satan had placed her finger on a certain night.

"The Abbe took another kiss, his hand passed gently over her thighs and slipping under her bottom, forced her to turn over on her side. Now he slapped her gently and pushed his finger into her slit between the two hills of her bottom, and it finally found its way into what appeared to be his desire to reach.

"But his hand set everything on fire on its way. With the other hand he unbuttoned his robe, undid his trousers and pulled out a prick whose erection was fully justified by the beauties his hand had explored and was still exploring.

"With a sudden pull, to throw off the cover, he laid himself down on the edge of the couch, close to her. Then, pressing her in his arms he covered her lips with kisses and taking her hand, placed it upon his god of love, firm and rigid as a rock.

"The contact caused the novice to open her eyes. He called her by the most endearing names: 'My love, open your eyes – kiss me. Open your eyes – receive my tongue – give me yours – so! Do you know what you are holding and squeezing so hard, my dear? It is the tree of life that you have so often heard about and desired so ardently without knowing the reason why. Place it where you put your finger sometimes. There! Not so quick! Open your legs... one minute... there it is!' and the enormous instrument presented its head to the little pussy as she instinctively drew nearer to the Abbe.

"He pushed gently, then raising her chemise, he uncovered her breasts and sucked them, bit them, then returned to her lips and with a shove he pushed his prick into its rightful place as he smothered a scream from the poor little novice. Now they are enlaced in the closest embrace and when his pizzle seemed to come out, she clung to him; when she seemed to recede, he boldly followed her up.

"He came out and went in; the action became accelerated; in her amorous transports she crossed her beautiful legs over his back and wriggled about like a dear little eel.

"'Go on, darling!'

"'Not so quick!'

"'Do you feel as if you were coming?'

"'Yes – it is coming!'

"'Quick! – your mouth – your tongue!'

"'Father – oh, how delightful it is. I am coming – heavens, how big it is once more.'

"'There!' said the Abbe, panting, as he gave a last shove. His engine disappeared in the tiny opening.

"Sister Clemence held him in a close embrace and covered his face with grateful kisses for the good he had done her.

"From this day on, the Abbe, who had found means of corresponding with the attractive novice, succeeded in introducing himself into the convent many times and Sister Clemence often found herself amorously wriggling under the vigorous pizzle of the priest.

"She received a thorough education in the Art of Love and soon recovered her health. However, this state of affairs could not last much longer. The Abbe was no more to be made a priest and reside forever in the quiet little village than was Sister Clemence to remain in a convent.

"The old aunt who had brought her up had been an invalid for years and finally died, leaving her a handsome fortune. From that time, the whole convent busied itself in trying to persuade her to take her final vows and give up her fortune to the community.

"The Prior even condescended to come in order to preach to her and the poor little novice was about to accede to their wishes, when the Abbe proposed that they should elope.

"One night he came to the secret door of the convent, carrying under his arm a bundle containing a complete suit of boy's clothing, together with a long cloak. Sister Clemence quickly put them on and together they slipped out of the place unseen.

"The novice looked fairly bewitching in her new costume. She spread her legs however a little too much in walking, and after hurrying along for a couple of miles, the Abbe proposed making an examination to see what the trouble could be between those beautiful legs of hers.

"He made her lean up against a tree and unbuttoned her trousers for her. To handle the lips of her little secret mousetrap was his only object, as you may imagine. He soon had her so excited that he was obliged to put his mouth down to it and with his tongue play a thousand amorous tricks.

"In her voluptuous transport, she sought with feverish hand the Abbe's fiery monster, which was only too gratified at being set at liberty.

Seizing it, she stroked it vigorously.

"To describe that scene would be impossible. The Abbe's tongue was well educated. Sliding between those rosy lips of her slit, it suddenly came out to circle itself into a multiple of tongues, so rapid were its movements.

"Meanwhile Sister Clemence shook his wand furiously, convulsively, and the movement of her bottom indicated that her delicious moment was coming.

"The Abbe's tongue went slower but pressed harder, and when she gave him a great shove accompanied by a warm rub on his immense cock, a superb jet spouted from the latter, while he received her little amorous dew upon his tongue, the deserved tribute of conscientious labour.

"That very day the Abbe cast his robe to the four winds of heaven and carried little Sister Clemence off to Paris. Once in possession of her fortune, she took pretty lodgings and furnished them nicely. She made up her mind to have a good time between theatre-going and her amorous sports with the Abbe, who had also a comfortable income of his own."

"The story of Sister Clemence is excellent, Mademoiselle," said I, "and I would give much to make her acquaintance as well as that of the Abbe. Unfortunately, it is only fiction!" I added.

"On the contrary, it is a story of real life, M. Dormeuil, the true history of a person to whom I can introduce you, if you like," replied the little woman.

"Truly I would be charmed to know her and shall await an introduction with impatience," I answered.

"You will not have long to wait," was the unexpected reply of the blonde. She then rose and making a timid curtsy, her eyes modestly cast down, her hands joined, she said:

"Allow me to introduce to you Sister Clemence, Monsieur Dormeuil," and she broke into a merry laugh.

I was amazed. "And the Abbe?" I inquired.

"You have heard me speak of Monsieur Lorille? He is the Abbe," she answered quietly.

I had a good laugh over the whole adventure, and then we conversed pleasantly on many subjects until we were interrupted by the arrival of Pauline.

Pauline was certainly a very handsome girl, very tall and graceful, with rich brown hair, large full, frank eyes and tiny hands and feet. She was Pauline for everybody here but Madame L. de Portiera for Parisian Society.

There were only a few privileged persons at the Hotel X— who had seen her face. This house was a particularly exclusive one, and only frequented by the elite.

Indiscretion was unknown there. Amuse yourself as much as you like and as long as you like but never overstep the boundaries of good society. Such was the motto and the rule of this remarkable house. A Minister, a Senator or a Prince could come here, give his name as Mr. Toto and if he wished to remain incognito, he never would be anybody else but Mr. Toto while he remained there.

A mask to conceal your features was equally respected. A great many persons wore them, especially the ladies. That is why, as I said before, Madame de Portiera had only been seen by two or three privileged persons.

A few widowers and old bachelors like myself allowed their own names to be used because they had nothing to hide; and they never had cause to regret it.

Pauline (we will use her nom de guerre) wanted to see me to request that I would serve as sponsor to a new guest. I accepted at once and to the usual observations concerning the person, she merely said that he was a Russian.

That was all that I wanted to know. Being near supper time, I took leave of the handsome brunette and strolled over to my restaurant in the Boulevard and afterwards dropped into the Cafe Parisian where I met some old friends, and someone being always ready to play backgammon, we were soon deeply engaged in a game.

It lasted until nine o'clock, when after a few minutes walk on the Boulevard, I returned to the Hotel X. The company was numerous although there was no particular reason for it, and I was soon quite at home with the joyous band. It is true that I often gave the signal for the craziest games and this was perhaps the reason for its popularity.

They were waiting for me. Pauline left a corner of the main parlour and came to meet me, followed by an elegantly dressed man, who at first sight attracted my attention.

A perfect blonde, with soft expressive blue eyes, he was my protégé for the evening and I introduced him according to the prescribed rules. He was received at once with boisterous acclamations.

The conversation of the Count, as he was called, had a rare charm that evening, and he spoke our language with great elegance.

In a few words I put him au courant with the few things he did not already know, and he gave me an idea to propose to the assembled party which seemed to me so amusing that I at once communicated it to the party. The ladies then surrounded Count Alexis and tendered him their congratulations.

It was some time since we had an entertainment and we were most grateful to the newcomer for the idea, which was as follows:

The next night there would be a ball and supper in full evening dress, and the ladies were to dress in gentlemen's attire. It was absolutely forbidden, however, for any one to wear trousers. A light gauze was the most that was allowed for the ladies' covering of the lower parts of the body. Everyone was to disguise his or her identity in the most ingenious manner possible and a mask was obligatory.

After arranging the details of the new entertainment, we separated and sat talking in groups and couples, the latter to give themselves up to the pleasure of fingering, almost always followed by a voluptuous coit in a little room next to the parlour.

END

THE ADVENTURES AND AMOURS
OF A BARMAID

A SERIES OF FACTS

Anonymous

1883

CHAPTER I

Polly D— is the daughter of an innkeeper in a market town in the county of W—. From the earliest infancy she was not less remarkable for the vivacity of her temper, than the beauty of her person. Mr. D—-, her father, contemplated with the greatest delight the growing charms of his youthful daughter; which, with a proper education, he thought when her person arrived at maturity, would be a most captivating ornament for the decoration of his bar.

Accordingly, at the age of twelve, Miss Polly was sent to a boarding school a short distance from her native home for the purpose of learning a few fashionable embellishments. After staying at this seminary a competent time, the lovely girl was returned to the longing eyes of her fond father, replete with every accomplishment that is in the power of those elegant receptacles of female education to bestow.

For a few months after the arrival of our heroine at her native place, her father gratified every wish of her heart; but he soon began to perceive, with inexpressible regret, the taste his fair daughter had imbibed for dress, and every other extravagance which young ladies, who have had the benefit of a boarding-school education, generally learn. He then lamented with the greatest concern the sums which he had lavished in the vain hope of making his beloved child a perfect mistress of the business of keeping an inn. Polly had an utter contempt for everything that was low and vulgar; therefore, the uncouth admiration of the country squires could not but be disgusting to her.

During the time of our heroine's being bar-mistress or barmaid, if the reader pleases, a company of strolling players arrived in the town, in order to exhibit their talents for the amusement of the country folks. Miss Polly was greatly pleased at this, for she had been once or twice indulged with a play whilst at school, and had, we must confess, a taste for theatrical performances.

The King's Head being the principal inn in the town, it cannot be supposed but the merry sons of Thalia made it a house of constant resort; nor is it surprising that, in their frequent visits, the greatest notice should be taken of the all captivating Polly. Indeed, the manager, who was a very polite man, soon made himself intimate with her; and all the hours that he appropriated to the drowning of care were spent in the company of our heroine. She had been long a stranger to adulation, and it is not to be wondered at if the insinuating eloquence of the leader of the sock and buskin tribe had not great influence over the heart of this lively and beautiful girl. In short, he prevailed upon her when the company was about to quit the town to accompany him.

Our heroine, no less delighted with the thought of "wielding the dagger," as of exhibiting her person on the stage before a country audience, the manager had not much difficulty in gaining her consent, especially upon promising that her first appearance should be in the character of Desdemona.

Mr. D—, being now quite tired of his daughter's extravagance, and she of the business of retailing, did not give himself any sort of trouble on her being supposed to have gone off with the player folks; but, on the contrary, to use his own words, "was very glad she had taken herself off."

However, the personal charms of our heroine, which were universally allowed to be inexpressibly beautiful, attracted the merited admiration of every lover of female excellence, her manifest deficiency in every part she undertook could not escape observation; indeed the manager well knew this, but it was the desire of enjoying the person of the fair Polly that prompted him to decoy the unsuspecting maid from her father's house. He had tried every art in vain to obtain his wish; and when he was fairly convinced the port was impregnable, he sincerely began to hate the poor girl as much as he had formerly loved her.

Our heroine could not but perceive this, which, together with the thoughts of owing a considerable sum to her landlady for board and lodging, and for which she had been more than once solicited, gave her some unpleasant moments, which even the natural liveliness of her temper could not at all times dissipate.

As she sat one morning ruminating upon these ideas, a note was brought to her in the following words: "Colonel H—-'s compliments to Miss D —, would be exceedingly happy if she will grant him an hour's conversation this evening, after the play is over." Our heroine, seeing a servant in a genteel livery waiting for an answer, imagined this billet could come from no person of mean circumstances; and as she was now really destitute of money, and her landlady become very troublesome, began to think that it would be the best way to recruit herself by disposing of that commodity which had been so much wished for by more than one, but no price, in her own estimation, offered any way equal to the value of the purchase. With these thoughts in her head she returned for answer that she should be happy to see the colonel at the time appointed.

During the whole time of that evening's performance our heroine's eyes were cast round the whole theatre in hopes of seeing her admirer. Her lovely bosom heaved with thoughts of a different kind from what she ever before experienced, but yet could not fix upon any particular person in the house to whom she might ascribe the note sent her in the morning. Her curiosity was wound up to the highest pitch; in short, she never spent so disagreeable an evening.

At last the time came. The fair one hurried home, threw off her theatrical dress, and attired herself in the most engaging dishabille. Her lovely blue eyes languishing with desire, and her snowy bosom half exposed to view, could not, she thought, fail of captivating any beholder; her thoughts were of the most pleasing kind. Anticipating the arrival of a charming, youthful lover, she studied to set herself off to the best advantage.

At length the wished-for hour arrived; a knock at the door was heard; she ran herself to open it, when, lo! How great her disappointment, instead of an amorous, impatient, lovely youth ready to spring into her arms —the fond idea she had cherished —she beheld coming into the room a decrepid old man, who, as soon as he was seated, began to open his business in the following manner:

"Your condescension, madam, in permitting me the honour of this visit, has made me infinitely happy!"

Our heroine was not sufficiently recovered from her astonishment to make him any answer. The antiquated lover pursued his discourse: "From the first moment I saw you, loveliest of women, I found I passionately loved."

It would tire the reader to repeat the conversation that ensued. The colonel said that he knew of her situation, and very gallantly offered to extract her, on the simple condition of residing at H— Hall, where she should be her own mistress; and, to avoid the insinuations of a malicious world, should pass for the housekeeper's niece; at the same time frankly confessing, "he was not able to pay his devoirs properly at the altar of Venus, therefore he hoped the lovely maid would have no objection to his proposal"; accompanying his solicitations with a pretty weighty purse. This last argument had more effect on the mind of our heroine than anything the colonel had hitherto said.

After revolving in her mind the difference between a starving actress and living in a house, though with a debilitated old lover, and under the character of his mistress, of the two evils she determined to choose the last; and, therefore, consented to his urgent entreaties, and it was agreed that the colonel's coach should receive her the following day.

We will pass over in silence the consternation of the dramatic heroes and heroines when they heard of the departure of their lovely and beautiful companion, whom we now behold an inmate of H — Hall; in which situation she was mightily contented for a short time. It might be here thought necessary to inform the reader why the colonel, who so readily confessed to our fair one that it was not for the sake of sacrificing at the altar of love that he wished to persuade her to go to H — Hall, it was more on this account — the colonel was ambitious that the world should think he was not so debilitated as was generally supposed, and that it should be said he had one of the finest girls in the kingdom then in keeping.

We will now return to our heroine, who, in a few months after her arrival at H — Hall, began to wish for a change in situation. She had heard much praise of London, and imagined, with a great deal of truth, that her lovely person would not long remain in that gay metropolis unnoticed. Being naturally of a warm constitution, Miss Polly, in reality, sighed to taste of those joys of which she has yet only an idea, and was firmly resolved that it should not be long before she parted with that, which, in her present situation, was a torment to her, though in general reckoned a blessing and a virtue.

The colonel had not been at all niggardly to his lovely mistress, but what he had bestowed upon her was chiefly for the decoration of her lovely person. The purse, the first present he had made her, was now almost exhausted. This made our heroine determine that at the first opportunity every possible means should be taken to fill it again, or to get another, and then to set out for London.

One night when the cloth was taken away after supper, the colonel and Polly being *tête à tête*, she thought it a proper time to begin her manoeuvres, as she well knew her old lover had that day received a great quantity of that valuable desideratum, some of which she hoped to obtain.

"My dear Sir, you seem a little fatigued; your tenants were so troublesome to you this morning!"

"Indeed, my love, I am; but I have not forgotten you. That parcel on the table is yours, my charming girl; so are these stockings; do, my dear, permit me to draw a pair on those charming limbs. Come, put your pretty foot upon my knee."

Polly did as she was directed. The colonel placed the candle on the floor, that his optics might be more capable of seeing his way; he could not help placing his withered hand above her knee. The touch was ecstatic — the stocking was forgotten — his pulse beat quick, and his whole frame shook; and while his rude hand advanced Polly grasped the purse, which the colonel in his agitation had left upon the table.

"Put it in your pocket, angelic woman!" were now the only words the trembling colonel could articulate.

As Polly removed her foot from the colonel's knee, one of her snowy breasts came in contact with his face. "Oh, heaven!" He said no more, and absolutely fainted. Polly was frightened, but her fears were soon dissipated when she saw her lover open his eyes.

"My charmer, I feel new vigour; suffer me to come to your chamber tonight."

At a reasonable time the impatient lover approached to what he hoped would be the chamber of bliss. Polly was a most irresistible figure, shrouded only in her chemise. The colonel had used the most stimulating provocatives, and it must be confessed that he had acquired a greater share of vigour than he had possessed for many years before, and was, with a little assistance, able to wage war with a willing victim; but our heroine was fully determined that her virginity should not be sacrificed at this time; having determined very shortly to bestow it on some more worthy votary of the Cyprian goddess.

As a merchant worth one hundred thousand pounds sometimes loses the whole in an hour, through the fickleness of one deity; so, by the precipitancy of another, did our old hero in one moment find himself robbed of all that store of manhood which had been accumulating for years back. Polly played off an evolution which answered her purpose, and which appeared as a perfect accident. The particulars our invariable modesty prevents us giving. Often since, however, has this charming girl, when her spirits were enlivened with the juice of the exhilarating bowl, related to her enraptured lovers the particulars of this entertaining scene. The liveliness of description and the warmth of colouring were expressed in such an animated style that her astonished auditors for the time believed the lovely narrator to be moved by the spirit.

CHAPTER II

Our heroine had now, by the recent bounty of the colonel, sufficient to defray her expenses to town, as well as something to subsist on whilst there. She therefore determined to engage a place in the stage coach, which passed by H — Hall every day. This being done, and having conveyed as many of her clothes as she conveniently could to a cottage bordering on the high road, she fixed a time for her departure. We will not relate the means taken to get away from H— Hall unobserved, or the consternation that ensued there when it was discovered that the housekeeper's niece had eloped; but must hasten to our heroine, who is now with a gay young barrister, the only other passenger in the coach, on the direct road to the great metropolis.

It cannot be supposed that this limb of the law could coolly observe the exquisite loveliness of his companion; he soon entered into conversation with her, and if he before admired the beauties of her person, he was now not less charmed with the brilliancy of her wit. Finding she was not averse to love, he plied her with the kind of language which a man that is long acquainted with the world knows how to use with success.

Our heroine was quite captivated with him, and as night grew on, suffered him to take a few liberties, which might have alarmed the delicacy of a more modest woman, but Miss Polly thought no harm in granting. The natural warmth of our heroine's constitution could not long resist the ecstatic dalliance which ensued without discovering those palpitations which to the feelings of a lover and a seducer are so delightful. Her watchful companion soon perceived that the wished-for moment had arrived, and without any further ceremony daringly advanced to the centre of earthly joy.

Modesty, or rather mock-modesty, gently resisted. It is well-known that in love resistance, instead of allaying, inflames the passions to a greater degree. This was the case with our successful pleader, for his presumption, had no sooner thrown his fellow-traveller wholly in his power than a large stone in the road upset his most devout intentions, and had he been on horseback, it might have been said that he was fairly tossed out of the saddle.

This sad discomfiture —attended with other little incidents, which we must omit describing, induced the barrister to make a speech on the inconveniences of stage coaches, in the conclusion of which he moved that the trial should be put off till their arrival in London.

London was not speedily reached in those days, and singularly fortunate were the individuals who could gain the metropolis without some little adventure. It was not the lucky fate of our heroine to miss a little affair which served at least to break the monotony of the journey. Soon after the incident related in our last chapter a party of gypsies were encountered, who encamped by the road side, presented a most picturesque appearance. Over sparkling fires pots were hung, and anyone near enough could sniff the fragrant flavour which rose from them, none the less grateful to the olfactory organ because the chickens which were cooking were stolen.

"Of all things in the world," said Polly, "I have dearly longed to spend a night in a gypsy camp."

"Don't talk of spending," said her companion; "it brings to my mind too keenly my disappointment. But it is a strange whim of yours, and stranger still that I have for years entertained the same notion. It shall be done! Gypsies are strange people, there may be some fun to be had with them. I don't know about stopping the night. We will at least make their acquaintance."

It has already been stated that our fair heroine and the barrister were the only occupants of the coach, no other passengers then could be inconvenienced by delay. A present to the coachman and post-boy soon overcame their scruples; their ready wit could easily invent some lie to account for the delay to their masters, and so the matter was quickly arranged; the coach was stopped, and young Capias (for so our barrister was called) and Polly approached the gypsies.

For a moment the natural timidity of her sex made Polly shrink from the swarthy figures they were approaching, the next moment she was reassured, for a young girl, with eyes black as night, hair dark and glossy as a raven's wing, and a scarlet shawl showing off her lithe figure, approached her.

"Tell your fortune, fair lady?" said she. "Can the gorjio lady stop to have her fortune read; the gypsy girl will tell truly what the stars foretell."

"You have just hit it, my girl," said Capias; "tell the lady her fortune. Show us into one of your tents, and as bright a guinea as ever carried King George's head shall be yours."

Thrusting aside the curtain of a tent, Mildred, the dark-eyed girl, led them into the interior. A great fire smouldered in the centre, the air of the tent was warmed and even perfumed by its smoke. A bed of heath and soft moss was in one corner of the tent, and being spread over with a rich scarlet shawl, it looked a couch which a gipsey queen would not disdain to employ as the scene of a sacrifice to Priapus.

Needless to repeat the pretty phrases which Mildred poured into Polly's willing ears. How she promised her all sorts of good things in the future, and then, with a meaning look at Capias, slipped out of the tent, so taking care that Polly should have a good thing in the present.

Before many minutes had elapsed the coy lady was spread upon the heath couch, and Capias was duly "entering an appearance" in a court in which he had not practised before; but which, as there was no "bar" to his "pleading," he contrived to make a very sensible impression. His few "motions" were rewarded with a verdict of approval; his "attachment" was pronounced a valid one, and soft caresses, murmured thanks, and close endearments rewarded him for his successful issue into the "court of love."

It did not take long to remove from their flushed cheeks and disordered dress the evidence of the encounter, and Polly and Capias issued into the open air to meet Mildred and reward her for her considerate attention.

The sounds of singing and revelry from a large tent well lit next attracted our lawyer's attention, and thereto he went. Around a large fire was seated a group which might well have employed the brush of Murillo or Rembrandt. The luscious leer on the faces of the men and women showed how keenly they were enjoying a highly spiced song of one of the company; and the right hand of most of the men, being hid in the folds of the drapery of the women, gave evidence of a desire to practically realize some of the stanzas.

A bold-looking, bronze-faced youth was singing, and the following verses give a fair example of his song:

Oh merry it is when the moon is high
To chase the red, red, dear;
And merry it is when no keeper's nigh
To trap and to snare without fear.
But better I ween is a night with my queen,
To lie in the arms of my love;
And to spend my sighs on those breasts I prize,
For a joy all others above.
Then here's to the thing that each woman doth wear,
Though we cover it up with our hand;
Its forest is hair, but still I swear,
'Tis better than acres of land.
I've sipped red wine from a golden cup,
I've handled the guineas bright,
But a sweeter draught from my Chloe I'll sup,
Her eyes give a brighter light.
Fd sooner taste the nectar sweet,
That flows from her ripe red------
Than I'd put to my lip the beaker's tip,
Though with Burgundy filled to the brim.
Then while I've a soul I'll go for that hole,
It gives me the greatest joy;
My pulses beat with a fevered heat
Whilst I my jock employ.
And when I'm dead lay under my head
A tuft of her fragrant hair,
In the silent land it will make me stand
As if my love were there.
Then shout and sing for that glorious thing,
That each one loves so well;

Keep me out of my meat, then heaven's no treat,
I'd rather have Chloe in hell.

Capias listened, so did Polly, with mixed feelings to this very irreverent song, but the night was wearing on, and they had some thought of the long journey before them.

Mildred approached Capias with a smile, and said —"The gorjio gentleman will not stop long in the gypsy's tent. Only let the gentleman be generous, and Mildred will show him and the lady a rare sight."

Capias was generous, and Mildred quietly led the way to a tent some little distance off.

"Step lightly," said she. "There are two of our people; they have eaten bread and salt to-day —they are now man and wife. Would you like to see the joys of their wedding night?"

Of course an affirmative answer was soon given, and Capias and Polly were led to a hole in the canvas wall, and witnessed the following curious scene.

At first only the dim outlines of two figures could be discerned in the interior of the tent.

"Wait a moment," Mildred whispered to Polly. "Gypsies always have a good light; no one would have his bride in the dark on his wedding night."

The peepers kept very still, and presently Mildred whispered again —"Zach is going to light up; you'll see him look Miriam all over before he really has her for better or worse, as your marriage service says."

The obscure figures now released themselves from a long embrace, the female giving an audible sigh, which seemed to give expression both to her amorous desires and timidity as to what was coming. Striking a match the swarthy bridegroom lighted up three candles, stuck in a common tin triangle suspended from the centre of the tent, which was a rather large one, set apart for the use of various members of the tribe on such special occasions.

"Now strip thee, lass, and gie us a sight of thy juicy koont afore I fook thee!" said Zach, imperatively. 'Thou's now all mine or now't, as I find thee."

Setting her a good example, he threw off jacket, vest, and breeks till he stood a dingy-looking Hercules in shirt and stockings, the former of which seemed anything but a clean wedding garment, looking a fair match in its unwashed tints to his olive-coloured skin.

She, too, was too dark for it to be seen if her blushes betrayed the shock to her modesty which the sight of his tremendous yard, the big purple head of which jutted out beneath that dingy shirt.

"Tak't in thee hond gal, and feel how randy 'tis!" he said, lifting up her smock the moment she stepped out of her skirts, and the pair could then be seen standing side by side in the full light of the candles, their lips glued together in a sucking kiss, whilst each one's hands were busy caressing the other's privates. She was a fine plump young woman of about eighteen, with a mass of black hair falling loose over her shoulders, but her lovely eyes were hidden by the closing lids, as if afraid to look in his face, or see her fate in any way.

"Oh! you hurt me Zach; did you think I'd lost my maidenhead?" she said, flinching from the insertion of his big middle finger.

"Thou'll do; thou's right, my gal. Now kiss my prick, and swear to be true to it, and never take another as long as you have me," he said.

She knelt down before him, and almost reverently imprinted two or three ardent kisses on the object of her desires, swearing the required oath in a peculiar kind of lingo quite impossible for Capias and Polly to understand, but they could see he was tremendously excited, for, lifting the fine girl fairly up in his brawny arms, he carried her to a heap of blankets, &c, evidently laid over a soft bed of ferns and heather, and falling upon it with her by his side his hands opened her willing thighs, giving a delicious view of a black bushy mount, with just a discernable vermillion slit at the bottom of the swarthy belly.

He was between those plump thighs quicker than it takes to say so, and throwing his body over her began to kiss her face and neck in the most passionate manner, being too long in the body to do so to her heaving bosom, which he caressed and moulded with one hand. The girl seemed instinctively to open her thighs yet wider, as he put the head of his tremendous cock to the small-looking mark, opening the lips with his fingers till the head got in about an inch.

Her hands pressed his buttocks down with all her force, and both seemed to quiver with emotion and spend at this moment, as they then lay motionless for a few seconds, till she gave his bottom a rare slap with one hand, and loudly whispered — "Try again Zach, my love; you did make me feel nice, as you spurted into me then; I shan't be so tight now! Go on —go on —Oh! Oh! Oh, oh, oh!" as he gave a hard push, sending his rammer in three or four inches, and then, before she could recover from the agonising pain, thrust again and again, clasping her fainting body (as she gave a piercing scream and lost consciousness) with his muscular arms, grinding his teeth in erotic rage, and behaving like an anaconda enfolding its victim, till his prick was sheathed to the roots of its hair, and dripping with her virgin blood at every withdrawal.

Polly and Capias were deliciously groping each other as they looked through the peep holes, but at this moment a loud burst of tambourines and rough music of all sorts arose from the camp fire, followed by a jolly chorus —

"Hurrah, hurrah, for the bloody strife,
That ends by making man and wife;
Hurray, hurray, she's a maid no more,
But a fucking wife for evermore!"

This startled Polly and Capias from their total abstraction.

"Ha! Is it like that with you two?" said Mildred, in a whisper. "I thought it would make you feel your feet again!" as she glided off into the gloom, and left them to peep and enjoy themselves all alone.

The noise and Zach's throbbing instrument in her tight sheath had now roused Miriam to life, as well as action, for in response to his movements she heaved up her rump and writhed in a perfect state of erotic frenzy, calling him to fuck her well, to shove all, all— balls and all —into her cunt, even biting his shoulder as she used all the bawdy expressions possible to think of. She was a demon at the game now, once thoroughly aroused, and to judge by her sighs and screams of delight was spending almost every few seconds, till she fairly exhausted her husband, who rolled off her body in spite of all endeavours to keep him on the go, and lay fairly vanquished beneath his rampant bride, who at once in triumph straddled over him, and transfixed his still stiff pego in her insatiable chink, riding him with all her might, till with an oath at her randiness he threw her off, and declined any more of it for a while.

CHAPTER III

Thus ended the episode of the gypsy camp, and our heroine with her legal friend regained their coach and continued the journey to town, whilst he related to her a tale of the seduction of two sisters, which by the assistance of a reading lamp he read from a piece of paper taken out of his pocket book:

"How very useful and contributary to seduction young milliners may be made, but in that and other instances we do not mean to cast a general censure; we believe that, notwithstanding a sort of lightness and frivolity, which are, perhaps, too often attached to the name of milliners, there are many respectable and amiable females who make that profession the medium of independence; and if their honourable, and right honourable customers, by paying their bills in a reasonable time, or at any time, would permit, the means of fortune also.

"The species of milliners to which we particularly and decidedly allude is that which in general consists of repudiated, cast-off, and kept mistresses, and make little more of the profession than finesse, and a gloss for the trade of seduction. Often have we noticed the street scenes, the nocturnal orgies of sensuality, the midnight immolations of female virtue, which are made and celebrated behind the shop doors of a millinery deception.

"In a retired part of Devon lived upon a very small fortune, Mr. Firman, a widower, a man of a sedentary disposition, fond of study, and, having experienced much of adversity, rather at discord than union with the world. He had been a Bristol merchant, and was growing rich when it happened that his six ships, together with most of their several living cargoes, were all destroyed within twelve months, and their owner in consequence declared a bankrupt.

"One was burned by a cask of spirits taking fire; another was wrecked; a third foundered; and a fourth fell a sacrifice to no less than three hundred Negroes, who in a frantic effort for freedom set fire to the magazine, and blew themselves and the whole crew up. What became of the other two was never rightly understood. We mention the reason of Mr. Firman's failure merely because he used afterwards to confess his misfortune as just punishment for being concerned in such infamous traffic.

"As companions of his retirement, as consolation to his solitude, Mr. Firman had two daughters, Sophia and Eliza, and a son, Frederick. The former were twins, about fourteen years of age, very beautiful, and otherwise endowed by nature. The latter, who had been left a small fortune by a maiden aunt, was also a very amiable youth, and intended for the profession of the law. He was about seventeen, and under the classical care of a clergyman at Exeter. Mr. Firman, though doatedly fond of his girls, was determined to send them to some respectable seminary of industry, and seeing a flourishing advertisement in a London newspaper that two young ladies were wanted by a milliner at the west end of the town, immediately wrote to a friend, desiring him to make inquires as to the terms, situation, and character of the advertisement.

The friend, without much attention to duty, made the business as easy as possible. He saw a large house in a grand neighbourhood, and was received by a smart woman, and to his shallow capacity that appeared sufficient.

"Mr. Firman received a satisfactory answer; for his friend, not only to prove his trouble, but his discernment, made the most of the account, and promised great advantages from the connection. The terms being reasonable, and the report being thus satisfactory, Mr. Firman immediately wrote to his friend, desiring him to conclude the business. His hopes were that his daughters would not only be the companions to each other during their apprenticeship, but that they would commence business together; and that as they had some very near relations in the fashionable world, they would make a flourishing fortune in a short time.

"As it would be tedious and melancholy to repeat the preparations, and separation of a fond father and his darling children, we shall pass over that series, and set the sisters down in Jermyn Street, at the house of Mrs. Tiffany, where one hundred and twenty guineas were paid as apprentice fees, and where the friend attended to see the indentures duly executed.

"The correspondence between Mr. Firman and his two daughters was for some time regular and reciprocally affectionate; but by degrees both punctuality and tenderness upon the part of the latter declined; they were so hurried with business, they were indisposed, or they were in the dull season of the year, upon visits to Mrs. Tiffany's friends in the country, in short, filial duty soon fell off entirely, and the poor old man at length wrote until he was tired to no purpose; they never corresponded but when they drew upon him for money to purchase fine clothes, and that they did oftener than his circumstances conveniently admitted of.

"It now became the time when the son was to leave Devonshire in pursuit of his professional studies. He was articled to a very eminent attorney in Gray's Inn, and had letters of recommendation to several persons highly respected in the law.

"Being settled, his first business was a visit to his sisters; the good lady received him with much kindness, but the Miss Firmans being a little way out of town, and not expected for some days, he was invited to call again. He particularly noticed three young ladies in the house, highly dressed out and painted, more like toy-shop dolls than as females connected with the humble and respectable occupation of business.

"Firman, though but nineteen years of age, and only just come from the most retired part of Devonshire, then formed conclusions not very favourable to them; and from the appearance of the place entertained very strong forebodings of his sisters' safety.

"Young Firman took his leave very much dissatisfied, but concealing his suspicions promised to return in a few days, and expressed a hope that by that time his sisters would be arrived from the country.

"Among other letters it happened that young Firman had one recommending him strongly to the son of a west country baronet, who, to qualify him for the bar, or perhaps the bench at Westminster Hall, was studying Paphian theology in Lincoln's Inn. He lost no time in delivering his packet, and as he was a very comely youth, and had a fashionable appearance, though innocent, young Mr. Thornback, the student, thought he would not disgrace him; that his ignorance would afford him subjects of merriment; and, in short, condescended to ask him on the next day, which was Sunday, to accompany him in his curricle to Windsor.

"On the road they became more intimate, and young Thornback opened to him the intention of his journey, which was to see a damned fine girl that he had in keeping in the neighbourhood, who unluckily he had got with child, and expected every moment would lie-in. Young Firman was too much of a greenhorn to relish this sort of visit, and Thornback observing him rather grave tried to cheer him by assuring him that his favourite had a sister, another damned fine girl, with whom he should sleep if he pleased that night, as she was then upon a visit at his lodgings.

"This did not, however, dispel the gloom of young Firman. A thousand thoughts of home, and of the new scenes into which he was entering made him appear more and more embarrassed; and they stopped at the gate-way of a very handsome house in the outskirts of Windsor, before he could recover himself sufficiently to make any coherent reply.

"They had no sooner alighted than a female servant, with a melancholy way-worn face, informed the Squire that her mistress was brought to bed with a fine boy, but added, with a flood of tears, that its mother was no more! Thornback, though a full-trained town buck of little feeling, was greatly shocked at the information, and a tear was seen to steal down his cheek, and on entering the parlour he threw himself in an ecstasy of grief on the sofa. At that moment the ears of the young Firman were assailed, and his soul rent with loud lamentations proceeding from a female voice to which he had been somewhat accustomed.

"Where is he? Where is he?" repeated the now well-known tongue. The door burst open, and the then only surviving daughter of the unhappy Firman, with hands extended, dishevelled hair, and distracted features, threw herself upon the neck of young Thornback.

"Surprise, shame, grief, and distraction, all uniting in the soul of the wretched brother, his emotions became too strong for his nature, and he sunk senseless on the carpet. The maid servants, who were the only persons in possession of themselves, assisted to raise him in a chair, and the noise and confusion occasioned by his situation in a few moments roused the sister —her transition was from grief to agony — from agony to despair —upon beholding in the person of a supposed stranger, whom she had not before noticed, that of a beloved —and as she thought dying —brother!

"From that moment she became insensible to everything around her —she became positively mad —and nothing but cords prevented her from putting an end to her existence.

"A few words regarding Mrs. Tiffany. She had been seduced at an early age by the assistance of a French milliner. After several changes she was kept by a West India merchant, from whom she obtained sufficient to take the house in Jermyn Street, affected the business of a milliner, that she might the more unsuspectedly carry on that of bawd and seducer.

"The two lovely Firmans were but six months in her house, and not quite sixteen years old when they were prostituted — one to a sharper and gambler for two hundred pounds, and the other for five hundred pounds to an old debilitated viscount."

As Mr. Capias finished the account of the seduction of the milliner's girls, they were already entering London, and were soon set down at the noted La Belle Sauvage Inn, Ludgate Hill, a hackney coach was called and Capias easily persuaded Polly to go with him to his chambers in the Temple. It was yet early in the day, so after a good breakfast provided by the housekeeper they lay down to rest on his bed till the evening, when he expected a friend to supper.

"Now darling," exclaimed the young barrister, throwing aside his clothes, "undress yourself, and let us enjoy without restraint those delicious pleasures which the accident to the coach interrupted, and of which we afterwards in the gypsy tent had only a rough taste. Ha, what exciting charms; let me caress those swelling orbs of snowy flesh, which I see peeping from your loosened dress. What a difference there is in titties, some girls have next to nothing, others are so full they hang down like the udder of a cow, and then again some of the finest have no nipples to set them off. Yours, my love, are perfection, let me kiss them, suck them, mould them in my hands!"

This attack upon her bosom almost drove Polly wild with desire, her blood tingled to the tips of the toes, as she heaved with emotion, and sighed — "Oh! Oh! Oh!"

He had gradually pushed her towards the bed, and presently when her back rested on its edge one of his hands found its way under her clothes to the very seat of bliss.

"What a lovely notch. I had scarcely time to feel what a beautiful fanny you had when I was so hot for the bliss in the gypsy tent. Now, darling, we can enjoy everything in perfection, and increase the delights of fucking, by such preliminary caresses as these, which will warm the blood, till maddened you beg me to let you have it at once, and my excited prick revels in your spending gap. And to think that I'm the first, that I took your maidenhead last night."

She was spending profusely, and begged with sighs of delight for him to satisfy her irresistible longings.

"Not with your things on, dear, off with them quick — see what a glorious stand I have got— there, caress it, press it in your hand."

He had taken off every thing, and helped her to do the same; then tossed her on the bed, and was between her open legs, as they stretched wide to receive him, but he toyed with her yet for a minute or two, letting the head of his engine just touch between the warm juicy lips so anxious to take him in.

"Ah, you tease! Do let me have it!" she almost screamed, heaving up her bottom, to try and get him further in. "Oh, do; don't tease me so," with a deep sigh, "I'm coming again! Oh! Oh!"

He awfully enjoyed this dalliance, but at length took pity on her languishing looks, and slowly drove in up to the hilt, till his balls flapped against the soft velvet cheeks of her rump.

"I like to begin slowly," he whispered, "and draw out the pleasure till we both get positively wild with lustful frenzy, that is the only way to get the very acme of real enjoyment. A young fellow who rams in like a stallion or a rabbit, and spends in a moment, scarcely makes the girl feel any pleasure before he finishes and is off.

"Many married women have stupid husbands of that sort, who never fuck them properly, is it to be wondered at that women get awfully spooney on a man who introduces them to the real delights of love?"

"Yes — yes — you darling —but push it in faster now. Ah, I feel its head poking the entrance to my womb at every thrust; that's so delicious. Are you coming, I'm simply swimming in spend. Oh, there it is, it's like warm lightning shooting into me. Oh, oh; don't stop —go on a few more strokes. I'm coming again. Ah, you darling. Ah —me! Oh!"

After this they had a sound sleep till seven o'clock, when the housekeeper knocked to say Mr. Verney had come. Thus awakened Polly was delighted to find the young barrister's prick still tightly encased in her tightly contracted sheath as they had dozed off in each other's embrace.

She wanted another stirring up, but Capias declined the retainer, and promised to make up for it at night.

"You're in luck my boy!" said Verney, as his friend Capias introduced him to Miss Polly D—; no other fellow ever has such luck as you have in the field of Venus.

"Her action is better than her looks," replied Capias, making Polly blush up to her eyes. "Nothing to be ashamed of, my darling, I always tell Verney all my love affairs; but don't you believe him, he's a devil for the girls himself, and one to please them too. Now for supper, she's taken all the strength out of me, and I want refreshing."

"Nothing like a refresher, after one good fee, is there, Capias. Ah! I wish I was you, the very sight of Miss Polly will make me uncomfortable all night, unless my landlady's daughter takes pity on me, and slips into my bed when I get home!"

At supper, and during the evening Verney scarcely took his eyes off our heroine, who could easily see how she had influenced him. Capias seemed anything but jealous, and paid far more attention to the bottle than to his new love, which rather chagrined her. Verney was a brilliant pianist, playing and singing with great feeling, and casting his eye on Polly when there was any suggestive point in the song. It was a a dreadful night out of doors, so the housekeeper was asked to make up a bed for Verney on a good wide sofa. He gave Polly a significant glance as this arrangement was made, and also looked at the spirit stand, to give her a hint of his plans.

CHAPTER IV

Capias when in convivial company was too much given to whiskey and water, which he took like a fish, giving no heed to the duties Polly would expect from him when they retired to bed. At length she said she felt tired, and bidding Verney good night asked Capias not to sit up too long, went into the bedroom. Verney mixed his friend an awfully stiff glass for the last, and as he swallowed it wished him pleasant dreams and plenty of fucking, adding, "I shall have the horn all night myself thinking of you."

The sot scrambled into bed to be received in Polly's longing embrace.

"Now, sir, you're almost drunk and sleepy, keep awake till I'm satisfied, or my name's not Polly if I don't leave you, and ask your friend to do your duty for you. You haven't taken a bit of notice of me all evening. Ah! you don't even stand," as she groped with her hand, and found only a limp affair for her trouble.

He was not so stupid, but he knew his deficiency, so taking one of her nipples in his mouth tried to raise the requisite desire, her fingers did their best to second the feeble effort, whilst his fingers on her clitoris aroused her amorous flame in all its intensity. At last he dropped into a sound drunkard's sleep, just as she was spending and almost frantic with baffled desire.

"You brute, you sot," she angrily exclaimed, pushing him away from her, "you're sodden with Irish whiskey. See if I don't keep my threat. Verney looks a fine fellow, who only wants a chance."

Springing from the bed, with nothing but her chemise on, she rushed into the other room, and threw herself into an easy chair, sobbing as if her heart would break, as she covered her face with her hands.

"By Jove, damn it, what's the matter," exclaimed Verney, as he awoke from a real sleep, and could just make her out by the light of the fire, so throwing off the bed-clothes, he got off the sofa, and knelt at her feet on the hearthrug.

"What's he done, to turn you out of the room, my dear, do tell me; I'd kick him into the street for your sake, Polly!"

"It's what he hasn't done!" she replied, sobbing, as he continued to ask the cause, and had put his arm round her waist, till her head rested on his manly shoulder.

"Oh, oh; I couldn't bear it to lie all night in bed with a drunken man. I'll get my clothes and leave this place!"

His hand was now up between her thighs, and his lips imprinted hot warm kisses on her burning cheeks. Higher and higher crept that insinuating hand, till he got fair possession of her chink, all moistened as it was with warm creamy emissions. She still sobbed on his shoulder, as her legs slightly parted, whilst a perceptible shudder of suppressed emotion told him too surely that his success would soon be complete.

Withdrawing his hand for a moment from that burning spot, he lifted her naked foot till it rested on his rampant tool, as stiff and hard as iron, as it throbbed under that caressing foot which his hand directed, so that it gently frigged him.

From her face his lips found their way to her bosom, and her sighs and oh's too plainly spoke her feelings, so taking her boldly in his arms he carried Polly to the sofa, and stretched himself by her side, with his tremendous truncheon stiff against her belly; he placed her hand upon it, and opening her legs she directed it herself to her cunt, and they commenced a delightful side fuck, their lips glued together, tipping each other the tips of their tongues; this made him spend in a moment, but rolling her over on her back he kept up the stroke, till she also spent in an agony of delight.

Resting for a few moments he went on again, her legs entwined over his loins as she heaved and writhed in all the voluptuous ecstasy of her lascivious nature, spending every few minutes a perfect flood of warm spunk, to the intense delight of his prick, which fairly revelled in the delicious moisture, which excited him more and more every moment.

Their bounding strokes made the sofa fairly creak, and anyone not in such a drunken sleep as Capias must have been awakened.

"Ah!" sighed Polly, scarcely able to catch her breath. "You beat him fairly, and I thought no man could possibly have given me more pleasure than he did. Drive on, push it in, balls and all —oh, fuck, fuck me. Oh! I'm coming again, what a spend yours is, how you shoot it into me, you dear fellow."

After this he promised to take care of her, and gave her an address where she could get two nice rooms, but persuaded her to lie down by the side of Capias again, saying, "And when he wakes in the morning, dearest, don't let him touch you —say no! You couldn't fuck me last night, and now you shan't again!' That will be a good excuse to leave him."

She acted up to this advice, and got clear of the Temple in a few hours, without the barrister suspecting his friend Verney had had a finger in the pie.

Polly drove to the address, where Mrs. Swipes, the landlady, said she was always glad to welcome any friend of Mr. Verney's, who was such a very kind gentleman.

Her new lover called in the evening to renew his fucking, much to the ever-randy Polly's delight, and left her several bawdy books to read, including Fanny Hill, The Ups and Downs of Life, The New Ladies' Tickler, &c; also three large and especially interesting volumes, full of large coloured plates, and every variety of erotic reading, tales, and songs, &c, called The Pearl Magazine which he assured her cost him £30. On taking leave after breakfast next morning, he particularly advised her to be guided by Mrs. Swipe's advice in everything.

"And you can easily be the best of friends with the old woman by indulging her love of gin every day, half a pint doesn't cost much, and I'll pay all your expenses. Be agreeable to the other girls in the house, and you'll be as happy as a queen; I'm not a jealous sort, and you'll get plenty of the staff of life!"

By this Polly guessed she was in a gay house, but felt pretty confident of taking care of herself, as she picked up a purse of gold he left for her on the table.

"My dear," said Mrs. Swipes, as she lapped her Old Tom, "gin gives one such an appetite, I can always eat well, but it's too depressing for men, takes all the starch our of their pricks you know, so never offer anything so vulgar to gentlemen friends, let them send out for champagne or brandy; whiskey, even, is not bad. You know the saying, 'Whiskey makes the love hot, and brandy makes it long.' For my part, dear, give me a man who can keep his place well, and go on with his fucking, getting stiffer and bigger inside my cunt, till he stirs my blood, raises all my passions to such a pitch, that when at length both come together it is really the melting of two souls into one, and leaves you to fall into that after blissful ecstasy which only true and experienced fuckers really understand."

Wetting her mouth with the gin she again went on, "Fellows who are so hot that they no sooner get into a girl than it is all over don't give a bit of pleasure – even some old men are so warm that they only require the sight of a pretty leg and foot to make them come in their breeches. La, my dear, you couldn't think what a nasty lot of fellows there are in London, both old and young men, who go about in crowds, or ride in coaches, where they can feel girls' bottoms, or tread on their toes, which is all they need to bring on a spend, instead of having a straightforward honest fuck, and paying for it, all the pleasure is had on the cheap. Never notice such fellows, always slap their faces. Now, my dear, if you would like to meet a real nice gentleman— such a handsome fellow too, a real Lord— lots of money, plenty of fizz, and everything jolly —why, my love, he likes to fuck me, old as I am, sometimes, as he says, plenty of good soup can be made in an old pot. Bessie Jones is awfully spooney on him, and he is coming to supper with us to-night if you like to make one of the party —what do you say, dear?"

"But how will Bessie like you to introduce me?" asked Polly.

"Do you think I'd have a jealous fool in my house? Why his lordship always expects me to introduce him to every new lady who comes into my house. Bessie and you will be the best of friends."

Here there was a tap at the door of Polly's apartment. "Come in," exclaimed Mrs. Swipes. "Oh, it's you, Bessie, is it; let me introduce you to our new lady, Miss Polly— ahem, what's your name, my dear?"

"Never mind that; what will Miss Bessie take to wet the introduction?" said Polly.

"I know what I should like to give her, and that's a good birch rod on her fat bum, for disturbing our quiet little con-fab," said Mrs. Swipes.

"Would you, indeed, you dear old girl, you do like to see a rosy bottom, getting redder under your strokes till the blood fairly trickles down at last. Stand a bottle of fizz, and I don't mind lending you my arse for a few minutes, it leads up to such pleasant sensations, and may be a novelty for our new friend Miss Polly; and I must apologize for my intrusion, the fact is I heard your voice in the room, as I was going down stairs to ask if Lord Rodney is coming to supper this evening."

"Fudge!" exclaimed Mrs. Swipes, "why don't you honestly say you guessed we'd got a drop of drink. I'll soon fetch the fizz and take the price out of your arse, my impudent, cheeky beauty, although I know you enjoy the touch of the twigs as much as I do the using them, the sight will give Miss Polly here a new sensation, or I'm no judge of character, she looks warm enough for anything!"

"Thank you for the compliment," replied our heroine. "I own I'm not a lump of ice, but make haste, I'm curious to see the birching!"

The landlady went to the cellar in person, and soon re-appeared with a bottle of true Madame Cliquot, in which the three ladies pledged each other "long life and plenty of fucking."

Mrs. Swipes had also brought with her, from the lower regions of the house, a long thin brown paper parcel, from which she unrolled a beautiful little tickle-tail, composed of a few long fine sprigs of birch, handsomely tied up with blue velvet and red silk ribbons at the handle end, whilst the tips of the twigs were so arranged as to spread out and cover a considerable area of any devoted bum they might be applied to.

"Lay me over the end of the sofa, and Miss Polly must hold my hands," said Bessie, slipping off her dressing gown, which at once revealed that she had only her corset, chemise, and drawers to hide her person, which was set off to the best advantage by pink silk stockings, pretty gold-buckled blue garters, and elegant high-heeled French slippers.

"As hard as you like, Swipes, dear, but you know I expect the gamahuche for a wind up at the finish."

"I'm all there when the tingling cuts make you spend, my darling, I wouldn't miss sucking up every drop for the world," replied Mrs. S., taking up the switch, as Bessie kneeled up on the sofa, and gave Polly her hands to hold tight, as she reclined over the round head of that piece of furniture.

The landlady now quickly unbuttoned the band of Bessie's drawers, pulling them down to her knees, and tucking the tail of the thin cambric chemise out of the way under her corset, both before and behind, so as to give a full view of a truly magnificent white rump, and all the stock-in-trade of a handsome and pretty young whore as one could wish to see.

"I'll begin as I mean to go on!" said Mrs. Swipes, giving a very spiteful swish to commence with. "How do they feel Bessie, dear?" followed up with a succession of sharp cuts, which fairly reddened the flesh of her posteriors, and made her writhe under the stinging sensation.

Polly could see as she held her hands how her face flushed at the first smart of the rod, then how Bessie squirmed at each cut, getting ever more and more flushed, as she bit her lips to prevent crying out. Polly could also very well see the reddening surface and rising weals as they appeared under the ruthless and stinging switches of the landlady, whose face flushed with delight as the flagellation proceeded. This made the blood tingle in the veins of our heroine, who quite shivered with emotion, and an indescribable feeling of voluptuous desire.

In about five minutes Miss Jones gave most evident signs of the approaching crisis, she closed her eyes, and hung her head over the end of the sofa, her bottom and thighs fairly quivering with the excess of her emotions, till Mrs. Swipes, throwing aside the now useless birch rod, rushed on her victim with all the energy of an excited tribade, turning the girl over on her back, and burying her face between Miss Bessie's thighs, as she licked and sucked up every drop of spendings from her victim's quivering quim, to the great delight and excitement of Miss Polly, who sat down and frigged herself in sympathy at the voluptuous sight.

About ten o'clock Lord Rodney was announced, and shown into the drawing room, where Polly, Bessie, and their landlady awaited his arrival.

"Strangers first," said his lordship, kissing Polly in the most amorous fashion, tipping the velvet tip of his lascivious tongue into her mouth as he did so.

"Look at the man, what a whoremonger he is, I can't have a modest girl in my house but he takes the most impudent liberties with her," exclaimed Mrs. Swipes. "How dare you, sir, thrust your wicked tongue into Miss Polly's mouth like that?"

"Mind your own business, you old bitch," retorted his lordship, a fine handsome young fellow of about eight and twenty, "or I won't lend Bessie my dildoe to fuck you with presently."

Supper was pleasant but soon over, and his lordship, who had sat beside Polly all the while, making her caress his prick under the table, arose from his seat with a yawn.

"Who'll take the horn out of me?" he exclaimed, "or will you give way to Miss Polly," he asked Bessie.

"With the greatest of pleasure," she answered, "only I mean to touch you up with the rod, so as to make you gallop, and not tease her with one of your lazy fucks."

All three helped to disrobe Polly, who was soon as naked as Eve when first presented to Adam, and they opened the folding doors into a bedroom, where she was laid down on the outside of the quilt, blushing and quivering with excitement as Lord Rodney, equally reduced to a state of nudity, got between her legs, and lay over her with his stiff machine throbbing against her belly.

"Look at his laziness," said Bessie, "he isn't even going to get into her when he knows she is dying for a good rogering — only wait a moment till I get my things off."

This was quickly done, and taking up a good thick bunch of birch, she let him have it hard on his brawny rump. It took a good many cuts ere he would begin to do his duty, but the effects were plainly visible on his pego, which stiffened and swelled immensely, till Polly, impatient for him to begin, took hold of it herself, and directing the fiery head to her burning slit, it very soon began to slip in, she was so well oiled by the anticipatory spendings she had not been able to restrain.

Miss Jones handled her bum-tickler with vigour, scientifically applying the twigs so that they not only cut well into his lordship's buttocks, but every now and then the tips of the twigs caught him well in between the tender inner surface of his thighs, touching up the rough hairy back part of his balls, and even inflicting little stinging touches on the lips of Polly's fanny, making her and his lordship writhe about and fuck away with a perfect abandon of amorousness, till the sheets were saturated under her bottom by the profusion of mingled spunk which oozed from her cunt at every thrust of his pego.

Now Bessie dropped the birch and, taking a huge dildoe from a drawer in the dressing table, fitted it onto herself, and proceeded to fuck Mrs. Swipes, who threw up her clothes and took in the big india-rubber instrument with the greatest of pleasure, as she reclined backwards on a sofa.

"Look, Rodney," exclaimed Bessie, "you can fuck me dog fashion, as I give the old bawd the pleasure she is so fond of!"

Thus challenged his lordship withdrew his still rampant and reeking prick from Polly's quim, and told her to pay his backside for the insult; then, getting behind Bessie, he clasped his arms round her loins, till he could frig her in front by getting his fingers under the straps of the dildoe, his well oiled prick slipping into her longing cunt from behind.

As for Polly this conjunction, and her still unsatisfied desires, made her so randy, that like a cow which wants the bull she clasped his arse in the same way he had Bessie, rubbing her spending cunt on his backside, and frigging his prick in front with her hands as it poked in and out of Bessie.

CHAPTER V

After this bout his lordship was fain to confess himself quite used up, but fortunately for our heroine, whom the scene had left in a state of raging unsatisfied desire, a late visitor to the house introduced as a friend, a real prince from the west coast of Africa, and they persuaded her to have him for a bed-fellow for the night. He was a real prince, and champion of love between the sheets, his tremendous pego was so untiring in its exertions that next morning at breakfast where they all met again, the landlady asked Polly, who looked a little blase, "if she still felt to want any more fucking."

"Good God, no!" ejaculated poor Polly, "his monster of a prick hasn't left a drop of spend in me, and he was coming again and again all night, and even just now would have another put in to give an appetite for breakfast; besides, what do you think? His prick is the blackest part about him, and it did make me love him so. White men are not in it with such a prince of fuckkers as he is."

Mrs. Swipes expressing her desire to just for once feel such a champion in her, King Cuntaboo was only too glad to oblige her, and Bessie afterwards, when he saw how her eyes glistened at the sight of his coal-black battering ram.

Lord Rodney and the other gentleman very much enjoyed the scene, handling his prick and putting it in for them, his lordship making some very learned remarks on the capability of the female organ to accommodate itself to the biggest pricks, as he saw how easily the women managed to take in all King Cuntaboo could give, notwithstanding its enormous size.

Mr. Verney did not appear a bit jealous, but, finding our Polly so well supplied with gallants, his visits gradually became more and more rare, till at length finding she was quite capable of taking care of herself, he kept away altogether.

She was such a favourite that in a few months she saved enough money to furnish a house for herself, and was so clever in her profession, as well as select in her circle, that she became one of the most fashionable and expensive bits about town. Noted for the extraordinary versatility of her ideas, every visitor to her cosmopolitan boudoir went away delighted. An incident in the experience of the erst barmaid will fitly conclude this tale of her amorous adventures.

Taking a walk early one summer's morning she entered Kensington Gardens and sat down by herself on a chair in a rather secluded spot, closing her eyes as various pleasant reveries floated before her vision.

"What a lovely leg! Alas! Get thee hence, Satan!" she heard ejaculated in low trembling tones, and suddenly opening her eyes, fixed them on an elderly gentleman, whom she at once recognized as a particularly pious Earl.

"Excuse me, young lady, I really thought you were asleep; may I present you with a little tract, it will show what dangerous temptations we men are subject to from the attitudes or coquettish dress of the pretty girls of the present day — do read it!"

She held out her hand and glanced her eye over its contents — as follows:

"Young women, your dress is often the creator of your thoughts and feelings. When modesty has presided at your toilette, the looks of men have neither the boldness nor the fire of desire. Kept within the limits of discretion and respect, they do not offer to your imagination the always tempting image of pleasure —and your sensibility remains in a calm, favourable to your virtue. A dress, calculated to inflame the passions of men, produces a contrary effect. Their countenances tell you soon what you ought not to be told. Why do you blush if you do not understand their language? How could you blush if that language did not force in your heart a sentiment it is not decent for you to indulge? When you are in a dishabille, that half conceals and half discovers your charms, you generally avoid the company of men. Is it virtue or fear that makes you so cautious? It is fear! You are conscious that, in those circumstances, men have over your virtue an advantage, of which all your prudence might not deprive them. Should Nature happen to be silent, vanity would speak, and bring the same rapturous confusion into your heads. The transports of a lover are so flattering—his admiration is so eloquent a praise of our charms —there is such a life in his looks and actions —we are, in our hearts, so inclined to let him praise and admire. Young women, I say it again, sip not in the intoxicating cup, turn your sight from it, in your flight only you can find your safety."

Her face flushed with indignation.

"Now, sir, where's one of the park-keepers? I intend to give you in charge for an indecent assault —you whoremongering, religious hypocrite. Now, which will you do, be locked up, or come with me to my house, where for a £20 note you shall have such pleasure as you seem quite unacquainted with."

His face turned white and red, and his knees fairly shook under him, as he stammered —"The sight of your leg quite upset me. I am so sorry if that tract has offended you; you must excuse me, I wouldn't be seen in your company; my reputation would be blasted for ever."

Then turning to go, but Polly almost brought him on his marrowbones, as she seized him by the arm, and hissed in his ear —"Where you go, I go — is it to be the police station or to my house? Expect no pity or respect for a hypocrite's reputation — what do I care for that after your gratuitous insult!"

The poor old man was lost, and making the best of a bad situation, elected, as a sensible man would do, to go along with the beautiful whore.

So finding him submissive she told him he could hold his handkerchief to his face if ashamed to be seen walking arm and arm with her.

They walked out of the park, and hailing a cab were soon driven to her pretty little house, but not before the pressures of her electrical fingers had already raised a cock-stand for the old man, who sighed and protested in vain against such wickedness.

However, Earl Goodman sensibly recovered himself as soon as the retreat of love was reached, and he felt safe from observation in Polly's elegant and luxurious boudoir. It was amusing to her to watch the variations of his face as picking up a decidedly naughty book he eagerly scanned its contents, at first his withered face flushed a little, then his eyes fairly started from his head, and she could actually see his old cock stiffening again in his trousers.

"That is the kind of book to warm up your blood," said Polly. "You seem to relish that kind of literature, my lord?"

"Humph! Awfully disgusting! How such ideas could be evoked from the human brain I can't understand —it's ruin to body and soul to read such suggestive filth!"

"There's no filth in the Bible you pretend to love so, is there?" asked Polly. "But how about Lot, Abraham, David and Bathsheba, Rachel, or Tamar, who played the harlot with Judah, Solomon and all his wives — besides, you know as well as I do, bawdy books don't drive religious people mad, or out of their minds in any way; used properly they act as a stimulant to the natural pleasures of love!"

Here she gave a quiet double ring, and a girl, presently entered as naked as she was born carrying a bottle of fizz and glasses on a tray.

"Oh! Satan! God help me! Not a drop, let me get out of this den of temptation. I'll write a cheque for the £20 —do let me go!" as he noticed quite a stern smile on Polly's face.

"Another insult, my lord —call Saunders and Ruth," said Polly, turning to the girl —"they will know what is wanted."

Earl Goodman fairly shook with fear, and trembled with fright as the cook and housemaid, entering their mistress's apartment, seized him like a child, and tearing down his trousers regularly spread-eagled him on a sofa.

"What are you going to do? Oh! heavens, she's going to birch me."

"That I am, and two gentlemen will see it all from behind a screen. When your impudent backside has smarted enough

I will accept your apologies and the cheque —but not for a paltry £20, mind —I don't birch an Earl for less than half-a- hundred."

He whined and begged for mercy, fairly screaming every now and then as the twigs cut into his tough skinny buttocks.

Polly was too clever, and enjoyed her profitable joke so much that she fairly wealed his rump, till the small drops of blood stood like beads on the broken skin; one of the girls was frigging him all the time till he spent under the extraordinary excitements he was so unused to.

At length Polly made him kneel in front of her, kiss the worn-out rod, and promise never to offend a lady again by offering objectionable tracts, and also to call and see her now and then on the quiet.

"My balance is awfully low; the late May meetings at Exeter Hall have quite drained my resources, and rents are so difficult to get in," he almost groaned, as taking out her desk she made him write a cheque on a blank sheet of note paper with a penny stamp.

"Thanks," said Polly, "I'll take a cab and cash it as soon as you're gone."

"Oh! pray don't go for it yourself, you might be known; send in some friend to the bank whilst you wait outside. Didn't you observe that I filled it up as if for the 'Midnight Missions,' as a blind?"

"Well," said Polly, with a smile, "you are a dear good old man in your way, and I will humour you about that, but I must say you have made a miserable use of a long life with good health never to have enjoyed as you ought to have done the pleasures of love —you shall have such a taste of it now as I am sure will bring you back here before long."

"You said your resources were drained, my girl shall see what she can do for you. He's in his second childhood, Sissey, so give him some titty, whilst Ruth gamahuches him into a rise."

His lordship had arranged his clothes before writing the cheque, but made no resistance to Ruth and Sissey as they drew off his trousers, vest, &c, till he was left in his shirt and stockings.

Sissey was quite naked, so she reclined on the sofa, and, taking his head in her arms, presented to his eager mouth one of her lovely small round plump bubbies, the firm strawberry nipple of which was indeed a morsel to tempt a hermit. She made him raise his shirt, &c, so that her warm belly pressed against his hairy bosom as he lay between her legs which were amorously entwined round his body.

This position left her bottom a little above his cock, which Ruth, kneeling down by the side of the sofa, took in her mouth, and titillated with the tip of her lascivious tongue. This lascivious attack on his virtue overcame him at once, so yielding himself up to the excitement he could not avoid, one of his hands clasped and pressed the young, firm, warm flesh of Sissey's bum, or groped a finger into her slit, whilst the other pressed and stroked the head of pretty Ruth, as she was giving him such exquisite pleasure with her tongue; how he sucked at Sissey's bosom, his mouth watering, and his prick gradually swelling till in a few minutes it rose a perfect monster to what it had looked before, and Ruth showed it in triumph to her mistress as she continued to softly frig it with her hand, whilst her tongue continued to titillate the entrance to the urethra.

"Don't you think its too big for Sissey, shall I let him have me?" asked Ruth of Polly, evidently longing to enjoy the fruits of her labours.

"No," said her mistress, "place it to her crack, she'll manage it, then take my ivory dildoe out of the warm water, and fuck yourself with it, as you sit in front of his face,"

No sooner did Ruth present the head of his machine to Sissey's crack than the lecherous little whore slipped herself down upon it, and assisted by his lordship's eager fingers succeeded in wriggling it all into herself, as she managed to slip under him and get him fairly on top in the orthodox position.

The old man was fairly carried away by his lustful feelings, and aided by the sight of Ruth working the ivory dildoe in front of him, and Polly's hands behind, as they handled his buttocks and postillioned his fundament— he groaned with pleasureable anguish, he had never been in such a tight cunt before, or felt such warm nippings on his pego, which seemed to grow larger and larger every moment, as it grew under the watering of Sissey's spendings.

It was too much for the old man when the final crisis came on him once more, he fainted from the excess of his enjoyment, and it almost took them all they knew to bring him round.

As a finish to this tale of Miss Polly's amours, it may be said that Earl Goodman, although very careful to preserve his reputation, often called to give her a cheque for the "Midnight Mission," and she actually got a little spooney on his grand old prick, which she said was such a delightful fuck when once fairly got in working order.

FINIS

THE DISEMBODIED SPIRIT

Anonymous

1883

THE DISEMBODIED SPIRIT

I found myself incarcerated in a beautifully fashioned sofa or couch, carved, ornamented, and made in the very extreme of oriental luxuriance; I was placed in a room in every respect worthy of my grandeur, and was meditating as to who was the occupant of this lovely retreat when the door opened, and a young Syrian girl entered. She was beautiful as an earthly Venus, with eyes large, dark, and dreamily voluptuous, in whose depths love had evidently as yet found no place. She was clothed in some sort of light, flimsy garment, showing the charming curves and undulations of her lovely form. She placed herself upon me, and gave herself up to her thoughts; these could not, I imagined, be of love, for she was evidently not yet fourteen, although (like all women of our sunny shores) fully developed.

After some time the noonday heat seemed to make her languid and drowsy. She disposed herself upon my luxurious cushions, and was soon asleep. Although but a spirit without tangible form, I had retained all the passions and feelings I possessed during life, so that the aspect and appearance of my lovely occupant gave rise to certain thoughts and feelings prompted by her beauty. I disposed of myself in the best position to see the still concealed beauties of my earthly mistress. For this purpose I first placed myself near the corner of the couch where her head reclined; here I could inhale the sweets of her delicious breath, and here I could also catch glimpses of part of her lovely breasts, as they rose and fell in the calm undulations of innocent sleep, rendered more and more excited by the partial view thus obtained, I longed for a more complete sight of these rounded globes; and whether it was that Minos took pity on my tantalizing position, or whether it was the result of mere accident, certain it is that she suddenly awoke, and, seeming to be oppressed with the heat, sat up and, quickly opening her robe down to the waist, fell back again upon me and slept.

Ye Gods! what a maddening sight now met my enamoured eyes as they feasted with insatiable delight upon the sea of beauties thus given to my view. Her rounded, softly moulded chin gradually merging into the white column of her neck, the last gradually swelling until it ended in two round, swelling breasts parted between, and crowned each with a delicious pink bud, their very colour (a dusky brown) but added to my delight. What tides of ecstasy thrilled through my maddened spirit as I wandered unrestrained over their soft expanse, as they swelled to meet my frantic pressure, unfelt, of course, by her.

I prayed in a delirium that through some mysterious power she should feel my presence and respond to my efforts, as I fastened upon her lovely mouth, and sucked in her fragrant breath; as if in answer to my prayer her face suddenly flushed, and her breasts began to heave with innocent dreams (as I thought) of till then unknown bliss. With what joy I saw her whole form, as it were, dissolve in ecstasy. Her sleepy efforts to respond to my fond pressures had somewhat disordered her dress, and I now perceived it had fallen from her limbs.

I immediately flew to the other end of the couch, and if I was excited before what must now have been my feelings when I saw her most secret beauties revealed in all their maddening luxuriance; her legs had opened wide, and as I gazed my eyes dwelt on each softly rounded limb from tapered ankle to glowing thigh; her hand, meantime prompted perhaps by some incident of her dream, wandered down till it rested between her quivering thighs, and unconsciously played with the short, silky, curling hair that covered that lovely spot. Excited or tittled with this unusual occupation, a pair of scarlet pouting lips opened, whilst the soft mound above thrilled as if longing for some unknown pleasure. At last she seemed to have reached the bliss she dreamt of. Her whole body heaved upwards as if to meet some responding pressure, whilst her breasts rose high and panted with the exquisite ecstasy of love's enjoyment.

At last, unable to bear the unusual pleasure, she awoke, her cheeks flushing, and her eyes half closed in languor, still disordered with the effect of her dream.

After some moments she arose, and whilst going to the door it was opened and a young Greek of about her own age entered. He was of faultless beauty of face and form. She flew to me again and arranged her disordered dress, whilst he, with eyes cast down, approached her with a humble apology for this intrusion. She angrily reproached him for the outrage upon her modesty, whilst Daphnis, with the deepest respect remonstrated with her for thus treating her betrothed husband with so much harshness.

Somewhat softened with his respectful behaviour she relented, and, upon his promising to take no advantage of her undefended position, consented to his remaining. Overjoyed at her unusual and unexpected compliance, he immediately forgot all his former bashfulness, and throwing his arms around her snatched a kiss; this seemed to remind her of her dream.

Her eyes again began to show a soft and melting languor, and although she apparently resisted his kisses, nevertheless she wished him to persist, at least she consented so far as to put one arm coyly round his neck, and now returned his kisses with responsive ardour, her feelings getting more and more beyond her control. Daphnis, seeing her bosom swelling with the excitement of his fond pressures, whispered softly a wish to see that lovely retreat of joys. To this she returned an indignant denial, but when her lover explained how innocent was his wish, that the married ladies of Resai exposed more than half their breasts to the gaze of strangers in the open day, why should she refuse her lover so small a boon? At this she seemed to be somewhat moved by his persistence, and hid her burning face on his breast.

"Well, since you desire it so much, if I show you as much as they show, will you be satisfied and claim no more?"

Overjoyed, and eager to behold what he had so often pictured to his glowing imagination, he returned an affirmative.

The lovely girl, blushing a rosy red, pulled down her dress until half of each glowing breast was exposed to his enamoured view. Maddened at the sight he embraced her form with frantic eagerness, and kissed them again and again, till, prompted by his unruly desires, his hand suddenly plunged between the panting mounds of pleasure, and took possession notwithstanding her resistance, faint though it was; for that unlucky dream in which she in her vivid imagination had already experienced, all this rendered her nearly helpless in his arms – both her arms were now joined round his neck, and lost in the mazes of her warm imagination she allowed his hand to rove unrestrained all over her lovely neck and breasts, whilst it now and then wandered to her waist and softly rounded belly (fear or ignorance kept him from encroaching further), her mouth half open like a ripe pomegranate, returned his burning kisses whilst her tongue darted between his lips. In a moment of forgetfulness she told him that she had in a dream admitted him to even greater liberties than these. This seemed to excite his curiosity, and he asked her what had happened. She said he had obtained much more than she would ever grant in her waking moments.

"What," said Daphnis; "were we in bed together and undressed?"

She blushingly admitted that they were. He asked if her feelings were the same as they now were. She said, between hesitation and blushes, that his hands had wandered all over her body, and that she seemed to be quite unable to prevent him, that just before she awoke she had felt certain pleasurable sensations it would be quite impossible to describe. His curiosity and desires still more powerfully aroused at this description of the artless girl, Daphnis asked if the sensation she had experienced was nice? This seemed to excite her more and more, nearly fainting at the very recollection, she exclaimed: "It was like nothing earthly!"

Eager to know all about this mysterious transaction, he desired to know what they could have done to cause all this, but some feeling of maiden modesty prompted her to withhold this.

Daphnis's desires had now reached a height entirely beyond his control; and indeed, she seemed to be in almost a like condition. They had accidentally slipped back on me till they lay stretched face to face; their bodies pressed together in frantic embraces; their limbs disordered. After some time spent in these efforts, unable to obtain the enjoyment of he knew not what, and, perhaps, prompted by instinct, he threw himself on her, clasped his arms around her waist whilst hers embraced his neck. Daphnis pressed closer and closer amidst humid kisses and soft murmuring, as if he wished to incorporate their bodies into one.

Whether by accident, or remembering the movements of her dream, her limbs by degrees opened to admit his body, twining convulsively round his loins. Nearly fainting with the unaccustomed ecstasy of their still raging, unappeased desires, they heaved and pressed frantically against each other with but now a slight garment between them. She could feel something pressing against the lovely spot between her thighs, as if it would force its imperious way despite all impediments, and with mutual longing it pouted wide at each aggression, as if it longed to admit the dear invader.

At last, exhausted with these tantalizing and ineffectual joys, they desisted for a moment, whilst Daphnis whispered,

"Was this like your dream?"

The lovely maid replied, "Not quite!"

"Why?" he asked.

"We were naked!"

This was just what he wished for, but had been too much afraid to ask. Rising, he quickly divested himself of his garments, and entreated her to follow his example; but modesty and shame struggled against her wishes, and, at last impatient of delay, he threw himself on her, and tearing forcibly her dress, the lovely maid's naked charms were exposed to his unrestricted view.

All thought of modesty or maiden diffidence was now completely overwhelmed and forgotten amidst the maddening thoughts of her unappeased desires. She sank on me, her eyes half closed with love, her breasts panting high, as if willing to be pressed, her legs thrown apart, impatient to clasp his body. Unable to bear the sight he sank into her arms, and lay for some time exhausted with the very fury of his longings.

She seemed disappointed and impatient at this delay, and pressing a burning kiss on his mouth, clasped him closer, whilst she whispered: "This was not all!"

Awakened from his trance at this fond invitation, he prepared to consummate their mutual bliss. She with trembling eagerness aided his awkward efforts.

The invader now enters the open gates of his longing mate, and presses onward – not without pain to both. Her breasts panted and heaved upwards against his chest, as each eager thrust sent a thrill of heavenly delight through her frame; her thighs quivered and clasped around him, whilst she seemed to dissolve in an agony of enjoyment. Now wriggling with her hands clasped round his loins, all at once they suddenly struggled more fiercely, clasped tighter and tighter, till with one humid kiss they sank fainting into each other's arms.

END

THE SIMPLE TALE
of
SUSAN AKED

or
Innocence Awakened
Ignorance Dispelled

Anonymous

1891

HONNI SOIT QUI MAL Y PENSE

CHAPTER I.
GENESIS

We used to live at the foot of the continuation of the range of the Malvern Hills, on the borders of Herefordshire and Worcestershire. That is, my father, mother, I and an old faithful servant, Martha Warmart.

Martha had been my mother's maid before she married my father, and was quite a confidential member of the family. Indeed, the idea of her leaving us never entered either her head or ours. Our other servants rarely stayed longer than a year or so because we lived in such a quiet hum–drum spot, amongst such perfect clodhoppers, that there was a scarcity of beaux; and what woman, saving a staid, elderly one, can be expected to like a place where the engaging male sex is so sadly wanting? Until I was sixteen years old I had lived in this dear old house, and so even and tranquil was my life that I never contemplated leaving the place.

If my father and mother had grown any older during those years I did not notice it. To me they were ever the same, and so indeed was Martha. My father was a great reader of books, much versed in science, and his delight and my pleasure was my being taught by him. Botany, geology, animal and insect nature formed the chief and most interesting portion of our studies; but history, geography, French and Italian also found their place. I learnt to play the piano from my mother, and altogether, though completely without society, my education would have done me credit had I had the advantages of a town maiden's life. As I have said before I was as happy as the day was long, never knowing what a violent emotion was like.

But all this was to come now to an end. One fine morning in the early summer – oh! I have cause to remember the 6th of June – my mother came down to breakfast without my father. She told me she supposed it was a long walk he had taken with me the day previous which must have tried him, but that he was so sound asleep she had not the heart to waken him. We ate our breakfast as usual, only taking care to make as little clatter as possible with our knives, forks, cups and spoons, lest any little noise might reach the ears of the dear sleeper above, and waken him from a sound and refreshing sleep. Ah, me!

I went out into the garden to see which new flowers had blossomed into beauty, and to pick a nice posy for my father, who loved flowers, when I heard my mother shrieking out for Martha. The tone of her voice alarmed me, and I flew to see what was amiss. My mother, seeing me rushing upstairs, called louder still for Martha, who came running as fast as such an ancient body could, together with the servants, who were as alarmed as myself, all with faces of consternation. My poor mother, seeing us all coming, went into her bedroom, and, pointing to my father, said, "I don't know what is the matter with him but I cannot wake him!"

I ran forward, but Martha pushed me to one side, saying, "Not yet, Miss Susan, dear!" and went and gazed earnestly in my father's face. He was lying on one side in the position of a person sound asleep.

Oh! He was dead! Dead! He had died probably very early in the morning, for he was quite cold and stiff: he must have been dead for hours. The agony of the discovery was unbearable. It was such a dreadful, dreadful shock, but what followed intensified our grief and horror, and made it seem as though all the miseries man was capable of enduring were being showered down upon our devoted heads. My darling mother never spoke again! She sank into a chair, gasped once or twice, and before anyone could run to her aid, she fell to the floor, literally heartbroken. I must beg permission to cease from any further details of the most excruciatingly agonizing moments I ever spent. I do not even remember how the hours, the days and the weary nights passed. I was stunned with the overwhelming grief and desolation that came upon me, and I can only liken myself to a happy bird, a native of the tropics, suddenly moved from its joyous surroundings to an Arctic desert.

The first distinct thing I can remember was old Martha telling me I should write to my father's man of business, old Penwick, whom I had seen several times when he came to see my poor dear father on business. I did so. Worcester, where he resided, was not very distant from us, but news from our part of the world travelled slowly along the country roads, and my letter reached Mr Penwick before rumour. The old gentleman was inexpressibly shocked and grieved. I find that suddenness has a great deal to do with feelings of that kind, not that I think Mr Penwick would have shown less sympathy had my parents died after a long illness instead of in the sudden manner that they did; but the blow, coming like a thunderclap as it happened, certainly caused him intense pain, and made his benevolent old heart open towards me in a most tender and fatherly manner. He advised me to think of some of my nearer relations, and to write and ask one of them to come and stay with me for a while, until some plan for the future could be made, for there would be some work for the lawyers, and much to be done before my affairs could be put into good order. I was a minor, too, and must have a guardian.

My father's will had to be discovered, and whilst all this was being done, as my presence was necessary, Mr Penwick said I ought to have someone to stay and live with me, to cheer me up and divert my unhappy thoughts into some brighter and altogether different channel. I felt too languid, too indifferent. My simple prayers were that I too might die, and go to that happy land where I had been taught to believe my beloved parents had gone, and where I might be with them for ever.

Had my cousins, the Althairs, been still at Leigh, Mr Penwick would have called in on his way in and out from Worcester, and asked my aunt to let one of the girls come to keep me company; but they had gone to live in France. There were other less well known cousins of mine, one of whom my mother had invited to make short stays with me some six years back. I did not care much for her, as she was a town girl, with ideas and pursuits altogether different from mine, and I remembered being offended with her for sneering, as I thought, at my 'beetle and pebble hunting' occupations, which to her were tiresome and uninteresting. Somehow her name came into my head Lucia Lovete and it was to her that Mr Penwick wrote. Lucia had lost her parents when very young; like myself, she was an only child, and she lived at Sunninghill with another cousin a little older than herself, Gladys Spendwell. In my heart I thought Lucia would never care to come, and I really hoped she would not. I was in that morbidly unhealthy frame of mind when it seems unbearable to have to speak to others. The only person I cared to see was dear old Martha, for she would cry with me, though she too, scolded me for not trying to bear up better.

But Lucia came: the moment she heard the dreadful tidings she left all her joys behind her, packed up a trunk and came as quick as steam and horseflesh would bring her. Nothing could exceed her gentle, sweet, sympathising manner. She took my heart by storm. It is true she was the means of making my tears gush forth again, but they were not the same bitter tears of desolation and despair, for I felt I had in her a true, supporting heart to lean on. Poor old Martha had indeed given me hers; but she was old, and Lucia was new and more of my age, being nineteen whilst I was sixteen. So to Lucia I clung. Shall I tell you what she was like? Lucia was just a little above the middle height for girls. She had a most lovely figure, with beautiful arms, hands and feet. The lines of her bosom were singularly beautiful, for she was full there without being too plump, and her breasts seemed like living things. She had a waist naturally small but not in the least waspish, and from this her hips gradually and gracefully expanded to a most exquisite fullness. Her head was small and beautifully poised on a throne of snow. But her face was too exquisite. Not only had she the most lovely dark brown eyes, most perfect nose, mouth and teeth, but her expression was forever changing. It was my delight to feast upon her personal beauty, and I knew not which to admire most in her, for each point seemed perfection, and there seemed nothing to praise at the expense of something else. Lucia might be compared with another girl as a whole – with me for instance (and I have often been taken for her sister) – but you could not say of her that she has lovely arms, feet, hands, breasts, etc.

I shall not refer to our dear Mr Penwick and his legal lore, for I am not writing these memoirs from what may be called a public point of view, but rather as a history of my most private thoughts, ideas and deeds, and truly I fear that Mrs. Grundy would never permit her dear sons and daughters to peruse so much naughty description as I shall have to give, however much she might like to have the private reading of it herself!

But of Lucia, and of the lessons she gave me, and of the practice I made of them, I shall write as fully as I can, nor shall I in any way allow my pen to be prudish. I am going to tell the truth, the whole truth and nothing but the truth, as they say in the courts of law, and as truth, to be truth, must be naked, so shall I be to my readers: and may there be many to admire my charms and appreciate them!

CHAPTER II
THE SOWING OF THE SEED

It was impossible for our house to remain long plunged in the depths of desolation, when once so sweet, amiable and lovely a girl as Lucia had come into it. Naturally of a most loving and sympathetic disposition, she had, at first, been greatly grieved at the sad loss she had herself sustained by the deaths of a loving aunt and uncle. The almost tragic nature of their deaths had also a naturally inspiring effect upon her, and she was as subdued and tearful almost as myself and Martha, but in less than a day she saw that if she were to be of any use she must overcome her own feelings, so as the better to raise our spirits. At first all our conversation was of the beloved parents, now, as I fondly thought, gone to eternal bliss in Heaven. Without stating her belief on this subject, Lucia rather encouraged mine; in fact she showed the greatest tact in gently leading my thoughts from the dark grave, and the darker secrets beyond it, to this world, and its multiplicity of pleasures and delights.

She insisted on our taking good long walks. The weather was open and pleasant. All nature seemed to be in accord with us, everything was well grown but had still to reach full development. We ourselves, Lucia and I, were in this condition too. It was impossible not to feel the effects of the lovely beauty of the country, of the sweet, fresh air and of the song of the birds, and with exercise came back a more elastic state of health, and as my body improved in health so did my mind. Lucia in old times had sneered at beetles and weeds and stones, and rubbish, as she called the results of my natural history rambles but now she appeared to take a delight in all I had to tell her about these things. I do not believe she knew a word of science, but she was so quick and intelligent, and seemed so anxious to learn, that I soon found myself growing quite excited in my eagerness to teach her, and if I referred to my dead parents it would be merely to tell Lucia what they had said about these matters, not to rail and lament as I had first done.

So some three weeks passed, and July was upon us with hotter sun and warmer air. We used to be glad to find some glade in the woods, near a purling brook, where we could sit or lie down on the grass and talk. One day when thus situated Lucia said, "Susan, do you intend to live here all your life?"

"Well," I answered, "I suppose so. Where should I go? and why should I not stay here?"

"Oh!" she said. "Now, my dear, without meaning to be at all rude to you, I don't think I could live here much longer."

"Oh, Lucia! You are not thinking, I hope, of going away yet! What should I do without you, my own darling cousin?" and I began to cry.

"There, there!" said she, putting her arm round my waist and kissing me. "I would not have said that if I had had any idea it would make you cry, darling. What I meant was, this is such a lonely spot! You never see a soul here from morning to night. I declare I have been here nearly a month, and except old Penwick, I have not seen a single gentleman inside the house. Are there no families with young men living near enough to have discovered the lovely violet called Susan Aked who hides her beauteous charms in these secluded groves?"

She spoke half in earnest, half in jest, so I said, "Now Lucia! Don't make fun of me. I may live in a very secluded spot, but I don't see why you should find fault with people for not taking notice of such an insignificant girl as myself."

"But Susan, you are not insignificant. You are perfectly lovely, if you only knew it! Now, let me speak! If you saw more people you could not help noticing, if no one happened to tell you, that you are beautiful. Yes, beautiful! Your eyes are something perfect, and so is your face. You have lips which no man could resist longing to kiss! You have a lovely figure and a perfect bust – or one which will soon be perfect when your breasts have grown a little more full. As it is I can see plainly through your dress that the high, hideous, stiff stays you wear cover two most charming little globes. Ah! Why don't you get others, like mine for instance, which give all necessary support without preventing the rounded globes being seen? It is really a shame to spoil a bosom like yours, and a girl ought to take care of charms which have so powerful an influence over the imaginations of men."

"Oh goodness, Lucia, how you do run on! Now do you think I care a straw for what men may think of me! As for my stays, poor mamma bought them for me, and I think she was a good enough judge of what I required."

"Ah! Bless you, Susan, dear! Now I would not mind betting that, had poor Aunt Maria lived to see you in society, she would soon have looked to your being dressed so as to show off all your lovely points to advantage."

"But suppose I don't care for society, and never wish to go into it?"

"Oh, but Susan! You are talking of what you know nothing about. In a girl like you society means great admiration, and who is there who does not like to be admired?"

"Well, I don't care about it for one!"

"My dear child, for you are a child and nothing else in spite of all your science and botany and stuff, you have been so buried here, that unknown to yourself, you have grown up in complete ignorance that there is a world of men and women about you, and that some day, perhaps not far off now, you will have to take your place in that world. When you do, you will, I venture to prophesy, very soon find out what a charm there is in being admired. But, as I asked you before, are there no young men in these parts?"

"No, Lucia, I don't believe there are. We lived so very quietly, that I suppose if there are any such creatures, they never found us out. Our parish is quite a small one, and, as you may have seen in church, there are very few people in it, and no gentry. Papa used to be called 'The

Squire.' "

"And you actually contemplate without horror the idea of living here by yourself all your life?"

"Oh, no! I hope you will come sometimes and see me, Lucia. I shall ask Gladys, too. Besides, I have old Martha, and I have my birds, and beasts and flowers in the summer; my piano and my books in the winter, and my poor people to look after. You have no idea of how very busy I am usually."

"But Martha won't be always with you. Gladys and I, I am sure, would be glad to come and stay with you sometimes; but, Susan dearest, I know Gladys well, and she would soon mope to death here where she would see no one of the opposite sex. Besides, her tastes are not half so countrified as mine, and I declare to you that, much as I love you, I do not think I could live here much longer without being tired of myself, and even of you. Women require men just as much as men require women. If you had some handsome, agreeable young squires down here it would be pleasant enough to spend the days flirting in the fields and woods with them, but there is not a soul!"

"My goodness, Lucia, how you do care about men! Now I declare I should not mind if I never saw another in my life!"

"That is because you have never known a town, my dear Susan. You have never known what it is to be wooed! You don't know the pleasure of courtship. You don't know what it is to have a man worshipping the very ground you have walked on. In fact you have never even dreamt of love."

I was silent.

"Well," she continued, "now have you?"

"I really do not understand a word of what you are talking about, Lucia. To me a man is nothing, and as for love, except for the love of my parents, or of you, or of dear old Martha, I know nothing. You mean something, I am sure, of which I have never heard. Of course a husband loves his wife, a parent his child, but I can't see what there is in such love for anybody to rave about as you do!"

"Have you never read any novels, nor any love stories, Susan?" she went on.

"No! My father and mother said they were foolish stuff."

"I have heard them say so. And have you not even Sir Walter Scott or Shakespeare in the house?"

"Shakespeare we have, I know; but it is locked up in papa's study, in the glass bookcase. I have never read it."

"Ah! Then read Romeo and Juliet, and you may perhaps learn a secret or two."

"The secret of love? But what is this curious secret, Lucia?"

"Well now, Susan, answer me. You are a girl, are you not?"

"Yes, of course I am."

"Of course you are! But why 'of course'?"

"Well, because I am, I suppose! I was born so. I don't know any other reason."

"But there is a very good reason, if you only knew it. Why should you be formed different to a man, for instance? Can you tell me that, sweet Susan?"

"I don't know, but what difference is there?"

Lucia stared at me with very open eyes.

"Oh, come, Susan! You don't mean to pretend that you have lived so long without knowing that there are most marked differences between a man and a woman?"

So saying she reached out her hand and lightly placed it in my lap, pressing her fingers on the part between my thighs. "Now are you not immensely different from a man here!"

Of course I knew I was. I knew that a man was not formed there as I was, but I tell the truth when I say I did not then know exactly what the formation of a man was.

"And have you never wondered why you should be formed here as you are?" she asked, keeping her hand still pressing between my thighs, whilst she gently stroked the place with her long, tapered fingers.

"No, indeed I have not! But, Lucia darling, don't do that!"

"Why not? You are a girl and I am another. Surely one girl may touch another there? What harm is there in it?"

"I don't know whether there is any harm, but oh!"

"What's the matter?" said Lucia, her colour rising slightly.

"My dear girl! Oh, for goodness sake, take away your hand! You are tickling me dreadfully! Oh, now, don't go on, or you will make me scream!"

"Scream away, my pet!" said Lucia, laughing. "You may spend your breath, if you like, but I mean to make you spend something else before. I have done!"

I did not understand her; in fact the pleasure she gave me was so intense, and at the same time seemed to me so shameful, that between the two feelings I was nearly distracted. In vain did I try to tear myself away from her. Lucia held me tight with one arm, whilst she half lay upon me, laughing and looking into my eyes as if she expected to see something she wanted to find in them. Very soon the tickling reached such a point that I felt that if I did not find some way of relieving myself I must faint. Lucia observed my rapidly weakening struggles, for she said, "Ah, my dear, if your dress were not so thick, and if you had not on two petticoats, I would have made you come before this; but I don't think it is far off all the same!"

As she spoke I felt myself, as it were, jump under her hand; a thrill, a throb shot through all that region, a delicious sense of some pent-up flood bursting the ever lightening bonds which had held it back made itself distinctly felt, and so great a sensation of delightful languor took hold of me that I could not resist giving vent to a grateful, "How nice that is!"

Lucia took her hand off, and throwing herself completely up on me, she pressed me enthusiastically in her arms, kissing me with the most passionate affection.

"Ah!" she said. "So my darling Susan is sensitive to pleasure! I thought a girl made like her must be. Oh, Susan, Susan, I would that I were a man! Would I not make you happy, and myself too!"

"Well," said I, "please do get off me, Lucia! I am nearly choking, and your weight; is perhaps heavier than you think. Ah, now I can breathe! Oh, goodness, I am all wet!" Lucia burst into a fit of laughter.

"Wet? Are you? Of course you are, darling, I have made you spend! But, Lord, if I had been a man, and had been slithering into you, instead of first tickling your cunnie with my hand, I would have made you spend a dozen times!"

"I don't know what you mean," said I, "and I don't know what you mean by spending."

"Why, bless you, girl! Do you mean to tell me that you have never tickled yourself there?" laying her hand once more an my lap, but taking it away again immediately, "in bed, until what you call the "wet", and I call "spend" came?"

"Never!" said I.

"Ah, that is just because your thoughts have never rightly turned to love, my pet! I really do believe you are as ignorant and as innocent as I thought you were only pretending to be! I see I have a great deal to teach you, and I will teach you, too! But see, it is getting time for us to be going home, and I dare say you would like to put on some dry drawers."

But although I pretended to be of the same mind, yet no sooner had Lucia begun to rise than I pushed her over and made a grab at her, caught her, turned her on her back, and putting my hand between her thighs, I began to treat her as she had treated me. Instead of struggling, she lay perfectly quiet, looking up into my glowing face, saying, "Well, what are you up to now, Susan?"

"I am going to punish you and treat you the same way you treated me, and see if you like being tickled nearly to death!"

"Oh," said she, "I defy you to tickle me. You don't know how to do it."

"Perhaps not so well as you do, darling, but I will try, anyway!"

Lucia had not nearly so thick a material in her dress as I had, and she had on the lightest of petticoats and shift. I could distinctly feel the soft, yielding charm under my moving fingers and even thought I could trace the deep line which marked her sex.

She lay quite quiet for about half a minute, when she suddenly gave a little start.

"Ah–ha! Miss! I don't tickle you, I suppose!"

"No, not a bit!"

I continued my movements. Lucia's colour began to rise, her bosom to heave; I could feel the elasticity of her breasts as they rose and sank under mine. I began to feel a fresh tickling myself, though her hand was no longer in my lap, and the caressing of the charming and beautiful girl began to fascinate me. Still, except that one little start, she showed no outward signs of being tickled by me. But all of a sudden she clasped me round the waist and exclaimed, "You have got on to it at last! Keep your fingers moving just there. Oh, my darling, my darling! Ah, that's it! Oh, Susan! Ah! Ah! Oh my God! Oh, how heavenly! A little quicker, darling! Ah, now, quick, quick, harder, harder, ah–h–h! Ah–h–h–h. There!"

The increasing excitement excited me still more. Whether it was sympathetic or not, I don't know, but as she exclaimed, "There!" I felt myself gone again, and a fresh flood once more soiled the purity of my drawers. I sank onto Lucia's bosom for a moment, and we both lay quite still. At last I raised my head and looked at her.

Her face was flushed, but she had her eyes closed and her lips slightly parted, and looked so still that I thought she had fainted. Alarmed, I shook her gently. "Lucia, Lucia!" I cried.

"What is it, darling?" she said languidly. "Oh, you dearest pet! What pleasure, what exquisite pleasure you gave me!"

Reassured by hearing her speak, I recovered my equanimity, and jokingly asked her, "Well, now, did I not tickle you?"

"That you did, darling, and right well too."

"But you defied me to be able to do so!"

Lucia laughed. She caught me again in her arms and said, "Ah, Susanna mia! There is such a thing as having a little fox to catch a lovely goose! But come, oh dear, I must have spent a cupful! I am drenched!"

"And so am I," said I, "for I spent, as you call it, again, when I was just finishing you off!"

Lucia, who was on her feet, once more caught me in her arms and said, Ah, Susan, to leave you here where you can never know a man would be to sin! You must come and live with me, and learn how to use and enjoy the exquisite and sensitive charms you are endowed with. You are just the girl to form into a real priestess of Venus!"

CHAPTER III
GERMINATION

We walked home quickly, my little terrier Spot moving close behind us, and sniffing at each of us, as though he smelt something very nice. Lucia laughed when she noticed it, and said he was a very sensible little dog.

When we got home she took him into her room with her, and I believe Spot had a very good time of it. At least, I know that on another occasion when he was in my room, he came whilst, I was changing my drawers and licked my cunnie in the most pleasant manner, a thing he had never offered to do before. Lucia knew a thing or two.

When I went downstairs I found Mrs. Warmart talking in a most animated manner to Lucia, so animated, indeed, that I could not but think she had been having a good glass or two.

"Ah, here the darling comes," she said, as I entered the room. "We were just saying, Miss Susan, that you are old enough, and big enough, to be showing your beauties to the world. For what's the good of a girl made like you hiding herself in the woods. You are getting old enough to be thinking of a handsome young lover."

"I dare say," said the talkative old lady, winking at Lucia, "Miss Susan often wakes in the morning and wonders where the brave young fellow is, who she dreamt was abed with her."

"Not she!" said Lucia. "You never knew such a girl, Martha! I don't believe she ever thinks of a lover at all! She certainly does not dream of one. Beetles and butterflies and old bits of stone are more her way"

"Ah, well!" replied Martha. "Miss Susan may have a butterfly yet for a lover, and I'll be bound she will find he has a good pair of stones with him."

Lucia burst out laughing.

"Aye, and she will like feeling and examining them too, won't she, Martha?"

"Of course she will, the darling! But look at the pretty innocent! She don't know from Adam what we are talking about!"

"Well, I don't," said I, "and what is more I don't want to. I detest the idea of lovers and should never have thought of such a creature, but for Lucia's chat."

Ah, well, dearie!" said Martha. "Believe me, woman's comfort and blessing lies in a man, and just as a man ain't perfect without his woman, so is a woman wanting until she has her man, to fit like into her."

Lucia clapped her hands.

"That is it exactly," she cried, "just like one of your beloved flowers, Susan, when the male part fits exactly into the female."

"I don't understand you," said I, bewildered. "How can a man fit into me?"

"Oh," said Martha. "Miss Lucia can tell you, Miss Susan dear, and most girls of your age would know it too, without going to bed with a man."

"The idea!" cried I.

"Well, when you are married, won't you have your husband in bed with you?" said Martha, laughing.

"I'll never be married!"

"Fiddlesticks!" cried Martha. "It would be a sin for you not to be married. You"ll never know pleasure without, and I can tell ye, young ladies," said she, sinking her voice to a whisper, "that until a girl marries a man she don't know what pleasure means. I've known girls, young ladies, quite afeared the day of the first night they were going to sleep with their husbands, frightened to go to bed, thinking something dreadful was going to happen, and next morning die of laughing at their odd fears, and long for night to come, so as they might have some more fun."

Old Penwick's bell rang and put a stop to Martha's chat, and I turned to Lucia and said, "Really, Lucia, you must tell me all about men and wives, and teach me, because I feel like a fool when you and Martha go on so. I don't understand one atom, though perhaps," I continued, as a bright thought struck me, "men tickle their wives as you tickled me this afternoon, and that is what Martha meant?"

"I tell you what, Susan darling," she replied, "I won't tell you now, but I'll come to you after you have gone to bed, for I don't want to chat on matters it would be difficult to drop, if that old lady came in suddenly atop of us. I think she has had a little too much to drink, and is merry; another time she might speak quite another kind of talk. But come upstairs. I want you to try on my stays, for positively you must leave off wearing such barbarous ones as yours, and we must go to Worcester tomorrow, and see what the shops there can produce, and if we can't get what I fancy there, I must write to London for some to be sent down for you to fit on. Such lovely bubbies as these," said she, laying her two hands on my breasts, "must not be squashed flat and displaced, but be left free to rise and fall."

So upstairs we trotted to my room. The first thing Lucia saw on entering was my wet drawers spread out on the bed.

"Good gracious, Susan! Why did you leave those things there?"

"Why? What harm if I did?"

"Because if old Mother Warmart should have happened to see them, her suspicions would at once have been roused, and goodness only knows what she would have thought – very likely that you had been had by a man."

"Well, Lucia dear, I am sorry; but indeed I never thought there was any reason to hide anything I did. I know you meant no harm, and I am sure I did not, when we had the tickling match."

"My dear, let me tell you that, although all the world does what we did, and a good deal more too, yet, just as our cunnies are covered up from sight, so are the deeds done by them. So we will put your drawers away. They are nearly dry, and if they stain at all, it will be very slightly. Martha will not guess the truth."

As she spoke she took up the garment, and held it out in front of her to examine its state of humidity.

"Oh Lord, what drawers! Why, they are only cut up behind. You ought to have them cut up to the waistband in front too, Susan."

"Why?"

"Because how on earth could your lover feel you if you had things like this on? Instead of finding a nice charming bush, and a hot little twat ready and eager for his hand and probing finger, this wretched calico would be in his way! And how on earth could you manage an alfresco poke if you wore these drawers?"

"Well, considering I would die sooner than let a man touch me there, I don't see it makes any difference. I am afraid I am extremely ignorant; but I don't know what an alfresco poke means, Lucia!"

Ah, well, you"ll learn, and soon too! I'll take care of that. But now off with your dress and petticoats. I want to see how my stays will fit you."

So saying, she commenced, with her usual agility, to undo her dress, and before I had got mine half unhooked, she was standing before me in her chemise and drawers only.

"There!" she cried, standing in front of me. "Look, Susan. Do you see how free my breasts are? Nothing to compress them. Each in its own little nest. They don't require support, for they are as firm as rocks, and hard as marble. Feel them!"

I did. Strange to say I had never seen a girl's bosom naked before. I had no girl companions, and the only youthful bosom I had ever seen bare was my own. I was immensely moved at the sight of the glowing bosom before me, so white and so beautiful! I put my hand first on one and then on the other of the exquisite globes, and felt a great pleasure thrill through me as I pressed them. Though not literally "hard as marble", they were decidedly extremely firm and elastic, and their shapes were perfect. Lucia was right to consider her bubbies lovely, for they were.

"Kiss them, darling," said she.

I did so with pleasure. It seemed to me as though some new revelation were opening up to me, for I never should have imagined there could have been anything so delightful in a girl's bosom, had I been asked about it, before Lucia exposed hers to me.

"Now, come! Quick! Off with that dress, you dreadful old slow coach!" she cried to me. "Here, let me help you."

In a moment she had me in the same state as herself. I saw at once the hideousness of my stays, which were much too high and much too rigid and which fitted neither breast, waist nor hips. Lucia quickly had them unlaced, and opening the top of my chemise, which she complained of as being too high in the neck, she slipped it off me so that it fell to the ground, and except for my drawers I was naked before her.

"Oh, the little beauties!" she exclaimed. "Oh, the charming, charming little bubbies! How nice, how firm! Why, Susan, I declare I should never have thought you had such perfections. Those beastly, disgraceful stays must be burnt, you must never put them on again.

"Bubbies like these," she continued, pressing them in her hand alternately, causing me to feel my cunnie tickling, all on fire again, "are not meant to be shut up in a box, but put under a glass case, so that they may be seen, and their full beauty appreciated. What lovely, lovely, little rosebuds. Like tiny coral marbles, topping little mountains of snow. I must kiss and nibble them."

And down went her lips first onto one, and then onto the other, whilst her naughty hand again sought the cunnie she had taught to tickle at her touch. Impatiently she tried to find the division of my drawers, and at last did so, but so far back that she could not get at what she sought after.

"What beastly drawers!" she cried. "But I won't be baffled!"

She ran to the dressing table, took a pair of scissors and, before I knew what she was at, she had the point through the calico, and had ripped it down.

Throwing the scissors down, she clasped me round the waist with her left arm, and again attacked my bosom with her lips, whilst her hand, having no obstacle to oppose it, took possession of my fleshy motte and throbbing cunnie; She was altogether too delicious for me to wish to oppose her. With the palm of her hand she pressed the rising, elastic cushion above the deep line, whilst her middle finger slipped in up to its knuckle, and was completely buried in my rapidly moistening cunnie.

"How nice! What a sweet, sweet little cunt! How velvety and soft inside; how quickly it responds to my touch. Oh! What would not Charlie give to get his prick into such a lovely shrine of love." She rambled on, moving her finger up and down, occasionally withdrawing it to seek another more ticklesome spot between my cunnie's lips, near the top, and then pushing it in deep, in and out, until I felt ready to die with the pleasure she caused me. At last she felt a convulsive little throb, which told her that I was very nearly come. She clasped me to her bosom, her breasts against mine, swerving her body a little from side to side, so that her bubbies swept on mine, backwards and forwards, her nipples catching on mine, and tickling them immensely, whilst with her lips open and sucking my mouth, I felt her moist tongue darting in and out between my teeth.

All this takes longer to write than it did to act. I felt myself growing faint with exquisite languor. I could see nothing. One vast pleasure seemed to embrace me on every side. I was all on fire, and suddenly, with almost a pang of voluptuousness, I spent all over Lucia's hand and wrist. Keeping her finger still gently moving, and gently pressing my motte, she drew back her head, looked at me and said: "Now, Susan, was not that a nice one?"

"Indeed it was," I said, feeling almost unable to speak from excess of emotion.

"Well, a man would give you fifty times as much pleasure with his hand, and a thousand times more with his prick!"

Then she suddenly left me, ran for my towel, wiped her hand and then commenced to wipe me gently between my thighs.

"Ah, what a pearl of a cunnie!" she cried. "What a lovely bush and what a lot of silky hair you have here, darling! What a splendid motte! A regular cushion for love to repose upon! So elastic, yet so soft! Gods! Why am I not a man now that I might enjoy all these beauties?"

"I almost wish you were, Lucia darling," I said, laughing, "for I am getting most particularly curious to know what new bliss there can be in store for me. But really! Do you know, I believe you are making me lose every particle of modesty I ever possessed?" And I laughed again.

" Ah, Susanna mia! Modesty is the shift which covers the cunts of us girls; a useful garment enough when we go abroad into society, and one which no wise woman would care to be without, but in intimate friendship like ours, it becomes useless, nay, like those wretched drawers of yours, and those abominable stays, all absolute bars to freedom and ease. I would not offend against modesty in public, but with you, or my lovers, I think it is a thing to be put off, and I like to be a natural woman on such occasions, naked as the ungloved hand. Ah, happy thought! Let us strip altogether now, and have a good look at the shapes beneficent nature has given us!"

She threw away the towel, and slid first one shoulder, gleaming like polished marble, then the other out of her shift, unbuttoned her drawers and let them fall to the ground, whisked off her garters, pulled off her stockings, and in less time than you could count to ten, dear reader, there was Lucia as naked as she was born, and as beautiful in her nudity as Venus fresh risen from the sea.

I, as usual, was slow. In every step I was hesitating. A struggle between consciousness and innocence seemed to occur every time I was asked to take a pace forward on the road to the fulfillment of the sacrifices to love, though I am bound to say that the struggle became weaker and weaker as every forward bound brought with it new and more exquisite enjoyment.

But Lucia could not tolerate slowness; she came and added her nimble assistance, and in a moment I was, like her, in a state of perfect nature. A kind of bastard shame, however, took possession of me. Not even before Martha had I been accustomed to be so completely naked as I now was, and instinctively I put one hand over my motte, whilst with the other hand and arm I attempted to hide my bosom. I felt myself blush, too, under the keen gaze of Lucia's beaming eyes.

"Oh, the charming, charming Venus de Medici!" she cried, clapping her hands. "Don't stir from that position, Susan dear, you are lovely, lovely. I want to walk round and observe and admire you from all points of view. Don't stir. Just lift your hand a little bit off your motte! That's it. Ah! I can see in you what that Venus was not permitted by her sculptor to show; the sweetest little cunnie retreating between voluptuous thighs, and shaded by the most silky-haired nest I have ever seen,"

And so she chattered on, walking round and round me, putting me into various attitudes and claiming, in what sounded like the language of exaggeration, at all the perfect beauties she saw in me. According to her I had the very finest shape she had ever seen; the glossiest, whitest, smoothest skin, without a spot, a girl could possibly have; a bosom for a god to revel in; thighs to clasp a Lazarus with and bring him straight back to life; whilst my cunnie was an object so perfect to outward appearance that Venus herself would have envied me.

All this time I was taking equal stock of her, and of her beauties. Ah, reader! Would that I had the pen of a poet, that I could do Lucia justice. I only half listened to her ravings about myself, so absorbed was I in gazing on her. Every movement was a verse of poetry, and every charm a blaze of beauty.

My room was lighted by one high window, and on one side of this window was the press in which I hung my clothes. It had a broad door, and that door was a large mirror, fully six feet high. I was a girl of nature. Had I ever bathed near this mirror I should have often seen myself naked reflected in it, but as a matter of fact, it never struck me that it was worthwhile to take the trouble to walk from the corner of my room, where my bath was always placed for me, to look at my naked charms in this glass. I used it occasionally when I dressed with extra care to go to church, or to go into Worcester, or to Malvern, but I was not much given to admire myself in any glass.

I had no idea that I was beautiful, and I did not care for my face. But Lucia, who was very artistic in her taste and no mean hand with brush and pencil, at once saw an opportunity for a pretty picture.

She drew the curtains of the window so as to form only a broad chink, through which light enough would shine to illumine any object near the window, but not so much as to cause any powerful reflections from the walls, and then placed herself and me, side by side opposite the mirror. I was delighted. I had never seen anything so perfectly lovely as we looked in that glass. Two naked nymphs with the most graceful forms, glowing with life, showing all that makes beauty most bewitching; rosy cheeks, cherry lips, glistening eyes, necks and arms, thighs of polished marble, breasts looking each a little askance tipped with rosy nipples, skins as pure as snow but lighted with the faintest rosy tints, as of light reflected from a dying sunset sky, and forms which shone out against the dark background, sharp, yet soft lined, and clear as the light of day. Oh, what a mistake artists make in failing to ornament the soft, rising triangle beneath the curve of their beauties' bellies, with the dark curling hair that Nature has provided, surely to enhance the lovely slope which leads to the entrance of the Temple of Love. The contrast afforded by this dark, bushy little hill, and the surrounding white plain of the belly, or the snowiness of the round, voluptuous thighs is really exquisite.

And why do painters and sculptors neglect the soft, in-turning folds, which form that deep, quiet-looking line, that retreats into the depths between the thighs, half hidden by the curling locks, but plain in nature, and to deprive woman of which would take from her her very essence? They don't do it to men. I have seen statues and pictures in which all that a man has, prick, balls, bush, are represented with striking fidelity, if partly idealised: why then should it be indecent to picture woman's most powerful charm? It cannot surely be said that what men most prize in her is too ugly to be drawn or moulded.

Lucia was wild over her lovely picture, as she called it. She put herself and me into various attitudes and admired, as indeed did I, all that the faithful glass reflected. I could not help noticing, however, that her form showed greater maturity than mine, but she told me that there were few girls of my age who could compare with me in that quality, and that in a very short time, some few months, my shoulders and hips and limbs would be as round as hers.

"As for your bosom, Susan, I would not wish to see it one atom more developed. I should like you to keep these exquisite little bubbies just as they are. Let them grow just a trifle firmer perhaps, but not one atom larger. See! A man's head could hardly completely cover one. They have just sufficient prominence to fulfil the law of beauty, and they look so imploringly at one as though to say 'Please squeeze me! Please kiss me!' Your motte I should like to see just a trifle more plump. Another quarter of an inch rise would do it no harm, and be more agreeable for a man to feel when he drives home the last inch, or squeezes in the last line after the short digs."

"I am beginning to understand," said I, "but Lucia, now you have the opportunity, and no one is near, tell me all about a man, and what it is he does to one. What are short digs?"

"I'll sleep with you tonight, my pet," she said, kissing me, "but I shall have so much to tell that I won't spoil the fun by beginning now. Besides, when once I get on that topic I shall get so wild, I know that nothing but my copious and repeated spending will relieve me, or you either," said she, archly laughing and stroking my cunnie most delightfully.

"Now," she added, "come, dress, and put on my stays, and I'll put on yours, and we will go and exhibit ourselves to Mrs. Warmart."

Lucia made me put on her stays and dress and she herself put on mine. We were much of the same height and build, only, as I have said before, she was everywhere a little fuller, more rounded, so to say, than I. Both she and I were surprised to find that her dress was not in the least too full in the bosom for me, and it was not simply the stays which made the fit apparently correct, for my own bubbies quite filled up the bags in them; in fact, had they been made for me, her stays could not have fitted better. But it was different with her when she put on mine. Her poor, darling, lovely bubbies were simply squashed out flat, and yet she could hardly get my dress to fasten over her bosom.

"Oh," she cried, "the brutal instrument of torture! I will wear it for a few minutes just to show Martha, but no longer. After that, Susan, my dear, we will change again. I wonder how you could have endured such a straitjacket as this, or how on earth your bubbies ever came to be so sweetly round and pointed as they really are. Mine are crushed!"

Then, looking me over, she exclaimed at the beauty of my figure, which was now shown off, she said, to perfection, and had a chance of appearing at last as it should. We ran downstairs to Martha, who, busy at some household work, looked up and mistook me for Lucia. Lucia was delighted.

"Ah! Susan, I told you so. Now look, Mrs. Warmart, I am not going to let Susan wear those abominable stays any longer. I know I have a good figure, yet just look at me! Did you ever see such a lout of a girl as I look! Positively you would never think I had any breasts at all, and I declare I hardly thought Susan had any either. Yet see! Just feel the lovely little ducks! Firm, round, elastic; such a pair of pretty doves with little rosy bills! It is downright shameful to crush them in such a wooden box of a corset as this. I know my breast is actually hurt under it."

"Well, you see, miss, it was all her ma's wish. She never liked Miss Susan to look grown up and developed,"

"But why? Why on earth? Anyone could see that she must be quite ripe. Look at her hips."

" Ah, well! She had a good reason, my dear young lady."

"Perhaps she had, and perhaps she had as good a reason why poor Susan should be condemned to wear drawers which must be exceedingly incommodious at certain times, to say the least of it!"

"Well, yes, miss. There was the same reason for that too. I hardly like to say before Miss Susan, because she is innocent like. Yet she ought to know to be on her guard."

"Well, Martha, since Susan is quite old enough to know what is what, you might tell us the grand reason."

"Well, miss, when Master Charlie Althair lived at The Broads, people said that there were not two greater pests than him and Jack Cocklade, who lived in Leigh. I do believe Master Charlie got credit for doing more than he did, but all the people complained that no sooner did their daughters get fledged than either he or Jack would be into them, and that ripe maidenheads could not be found, high or low! What Master Charlie did not pluck, Jack did. No one ever brought an affiliation case against Master Charlie, but Jack is known to be father of ever so many love children. Poor Miss Mary Essex was raped by one or other of 'em in her own father's field, not half a mile from home. I believe that it was Jack who did it, but there was a great noise a little time after when she and Master Charlie were caught hard at it by Mr Essex in one of his barns. They were caught in the very act, and it was that which caused Mrs. Althair, who had no idea until then what a lively lad he was, to go away from The Broads. I believe she had to pay up handsomely for that little spree of her son's, and being a very strict and straight lady, she could not face the people after her disgrace, as she called it. Jack, indeed, got imprisoned for his share, because Miss Mary Essex confessed he had had her before Master Charlie and against her will; but Master Charlie was let off pretty easy because she had to admit that she did love being had by him. This happened some five or six years ago, and poor Mrs. Aked got such a shock she wouldn't let Miss Susan out by herself, nor allow her to have her drawers divided at all. But poor Miss Susan complained she could not do her jobs easy when she had to unbutton her drawers behind, so she had them cut as you find them now."

I saw that Lucia was shaking with internal laughter, and I felt beetroot–red with shame. But more and more I understood what was said about Charlie Althair and Jack Cocklade, and why my drawers were so made as to cover my cunnie completely when not partly loosened.

"Well, Martha," said Lucia, "I think Susan can defend herself in future. So anyhow I am going to take it on myself to drive her to Worcester tomorrow to look for a decent pair of stays, and as she is so uncomfortable in her drawers, we will cut them up in front and make them as they should be."

"I"m much afraid you can't go to Worcester tomorrow, my dear young lady, because the horse has gone to be shod, and won't be back till tomorrow afternoon. Bill Coachman is going to Hereford to see his wife's mother, and said he would not be here till tomorrow evening, but the brougham will be ready for you the next day after."

"Well, so be it. We can wait a day. Come, Susan. Now for goodness" sake let me have my stays again!"

So off we trotted upstairs once more. I admired myself in the glass until Lucia had taken off her dress, and then, with a sigh, I yielded her own, and once more clad myself in my old habiliments.

Agreeably to her promise Lucia came to my bedroom after Martha and the servants had gone to bed. She sprang into my bed and clasped me in her arms and kissed me repeatedly and said, "Oh, Susan, we will have such a night of it. I'll tell you all you want to know, and I will show you more, and I will prove to you that it is downright folly to lose years of youth, which can be so well turned to profit by using the charms and senses nature has given you. But let me put my hand between your legs, darling. Ah, that is it. Now I'll just slip my finger in this delicious little cunt. You do the same to me!"

" Ah! Now am I not nice and hot and soft inside?"

"Indeed you are, Lucia, like velvet warmed before the fire."

"And so are you, darling; but now we won't have any tickling yet. Now I will tell you about men."

"Oh, do! I am dying with curiosity, Lucia."

"Well now, just here," said she, pressing her thumb on a spot above my cunnie, "a man's thing grows out from him. That thing is called his prick, or his yard, or his tool, or his Johnnie, or half a hundred other names. When it is not standing, it is about two and a half or three inches long, all small and soft and flabby and wrinkled, but when it stands it is seven or eight inches long, as big round as my wrist, and hard as iron. A most formidable weapon to thrust into the poor little belly of a girl!"

"But what makes it stand, Lucia?" I asked, breathless with unaccountable emotion, and feeling a strange shiver pass through me at the notion of such a monstrous thing being thrust into my belly.

"Oh, there are physical reasons for that which I won't go into now, but the actual cause of its standing is desire. When a man thinks of a girl and wants to have her, up goes his prick; it lifts itself with pride and power, and becomes just like a bar of iron covered from end to end with a thick, soft, velvety skin. If you were to take a good hold of one in that condition you could move your hand up and down, without the skin slipping from under your fingers, just like you can move the skin of a cat on its body!"

"Really? How curious!"

"Yes, well, there it stands. But it is not exactly round. It is slightly broader than it is deep, so to say, and it has the most curious-looking head imaginable. It is something like a cherry at the end, and in the tip is a little hole, out of which comes the dangerous stuff which makes the little babies!"

"Oh, my!"

"Well, the head is shaped there like a bell. It is bluish purple round the lower rim, which rim forms a regular shoulder. You can slip the moveable skin right off the head and behind the shoulder, and there it will stay, unless it is forcibly put back again. Underneath the nose, as I will take it, of the prick, the moveable skin is fastened, not far behind the point, and when the stand or stiffness is gone out of the prick this fastening pulls the cap over its head again!"

"How very curious! How convenient!"

"Well, now. Under the prick, nearly as far back, but not quite, as the place where it springs from, is a very curious, very wrinkled bag, in which the balls are – balls something like small eggs, and far nicer both to feel and see. I dearly love feeling a man's balls, and does not he like it too? They feel slippery and hard, but you must take care not to squeeze them tight, as it hurts a man very much; but gently handling them, lifting them up with the tips of the fingers, and gently rolling them about in their bag, is most pleasing to every man, and if his prick has gone down, such treatment will quickly bring it back grand and stiff and big and ready for work again."

"And what are his balls for, Lucia?" said I.

"Oh! His balls hold the stuff he spends when he fucks us, darling. A white, creamy looking stuff, like milk only thicker, which spouts out in jets. I have seen Charlie Althair spout it three feet high."

"Charlie Althair!" I exclaimed.

"Yes, darling. Charlie was my first love, and it was he who took my maidenhead. He is a grand fellow everywhere, and no girl could have him in her bed without going half mad over him. He is able to give extraordinary pleasure, and I ought to know, for I have had plenty of experience."

"Then there is a difference between men that way, Lucia?"

"Oh, there is indeed! Sometimes one gets hold of a fellow, well made in every respect, but an indifferent bedfellow, not simply because he does not, or cannot give one enough, but because he does not know how to do it properly."

" And how should it be done properly, Lucia?"

"I'll tell you, darling. Oh, if I only were a man! If only instead of this cunt I had a rattling, fine, big, long prick, as stiff as a poker, and a well furnished pair of balls hanging to it, I would show you, my Susan! I would show you what a real, good, unmistakeable fuck is! I am just the one who knows how it should be done, to be well done."

" Ah, Lucia; but as you have no prick, and no balls, can't you tell me all the same? I am dying to know."

" Ah, my sweet Susan is growing randy! I know she is. I think a little bit of a spend would do her good! I tell you what," she said, her voice growing thick and hurried, as though emotion were choking her, "I will show you how a man gets onto you, and how he moves, and I will make you spend a dozen times, for, darling, I must either spend myself or burst!"

So saying, she pulled my chemise above my bubbies, and rolled it on my neck, and pulling up her own, and holding its end under her chin and on her bosom, she got between my knees.

"Open your thighs wide, darling, my darling!" she cried in a most excited manner. "Open your thighs! Draw up your knees! That is it. Oh, my! A kingdom to have a prick now!"

She sank onto my belly. She put one hand under my hips to raise them. The other she put round my neck. Her bubbies coincided with mine, and I could feel their hard little nipples pressing into my breasts, whilst mine, equally hard, met her harder and more elastic globes. She pressed her bushy motte to mine, lifted me a little with her hand, and brought the two hot lips of her burning cunnie onto mine. Then she sank her hips. The top of her cunt touched the bottom of mine, and then with a pressing upward sweep, she brought her cunnie all over mine from end to end of the slit.

Down she swept again! Then up, then down, until I thrilled through and through with extraordinary and untold pleasure. I felt her grasp growing tighter and tighter, as her breathing became more and more hurried. Her breasts crushed mine, and they seemed to swell and become harder. Then, when she had come to the end of one of her long upward sweeps, she suddenly spent all over my motte. I could feel the hair there inundated. At the same moment she received my offering full on her cunnie as she swept down mine. This excited her immensely, and she redoubled her efforts to make the spasms come again. I clasped her to me. I returned the rain of furnace-like kisses she showered all over my face. I felt wild. Again and again we spent all over one another's cunts and bushes, I can't tell how many times, until at length drenched, breathless and tired, Lucia lay heavily on me, and for a moment we were motionless. Then, lifting her head, she kissed me in the most loving manner.

"My little darling! My own sweetest, darling Susan! how did you like that?"

"Oh, Lucia, it was heavenly! Do it again, darling!" I cried, clasping her between my thighs, and pressing my glowing cunt to hers.

"Not just yet, dearest! No, Susan, I have come at least fifteen times, and you are wet as a drowned rat! Indeed so am I, you naughty little girl! How you do spend!"

"You taught me," said I.

"Ah, yes! You are a darling and splendid pupil, my Susan, and a perfect mine of these pearls!" said she, pointing to a drop depending from her bush which, when it dropped onto my thigh as she got off me, felt cold.

"Now," she continued, "Come, get up! We must ablutionise."

We both got out of bed. Lucia dropped her chemise and stood naked and beautiful before me. I did the same. She again exclaimed at what she called the extraordinary gracefulness of my figure, and again wished she was a man.

We washed one another's cunnies, and then, naked as we were, again got into bed, and with arms round one another's waists, and thighs locked in thighs, we pressed our bosoms together, and Lucia continued her instructions.

"Well, Susanna mia, that little bit of initiation was a nice interlude, and imperfect as it was, it has shown you at least how you will have to lie when you are had, a la Adam and Eve, by a man, for you must not imagine for a moment that a man has only one way of fucking a girl. There are heaps of ways, all more or less nice, but to my simple mind the Adam and Eve is the best of all, because it is the most natural and the most perfect."

"But, Lucia darling," said I, "I have not a notion of what you mean by "Adam and Eve" as compared with other ways. You said you would tell me how a man should well do it with a girl, so as to be perfect in his action."

"Oh, my modest little mouse! Now, Susan, say "fuck"."

"I was not quite sure of the term, Lucia dearest. I did not mean to be over-particular. Well, tell me exactly how a man should fuck a girl, so as to give her the most complete pleasure. For my part, not knowing what it is like, I should imagine that the mere sensation of having so big a thing as you say a man's prick is, inside one's cunt, would be rather disagreeable than otherwise. Why, even you, who have, you tell me, been fucked, have quite a tight little cunt. How on earth can such a small, narrow slit like this take in a thing as thick as one's wrist? I can hardly believe it or, if I do believe it, I can hardly fancy its being pleasant."

Lucia listened to me with a smiling face. She kissed me, and put her hand on my motte, slipping her finger up to her knuckles into my still throbbing cunnie.

"Yes, my Susan. Our cunts are, luckily for us and our lovers, small and tight. If they were not, neither they nor we would have half the pleasure we do. I say we, because it won't be long now before you know what a delicious, deliriously rapturous and excessively delightful thing it is to be well and often fucked. Oh dear, why have I not a prick? How easy it would be to show you, darling; far more easy than to explain!"

"Oh, Lucia do go on! Tell me, girl you keep me actually on thorns of expectation!"

Lucia laughed, passed her finger deliciously two or three times up and down my cunnie, then took it out, and grasped my left breast in her hand, pressing it gently, as though she loved doing so.

"Well, Susan, here it goes. Now I'll do my best to describe what a man should do to give you the acme of pleasure. First of all he should put his prick into your hand. It is a most thrilling thing to feel; oh, it is delightful when you feel it from end to end. Its hardness like iron; its soft velvety skin, its soft cushion-like head and its shifting hood; his grand balls in their wrinkled, silky, soft bag; and the thick, rough bush out of which this galaxy of manly charms grows, all form objects of delight to the hand that knows how to caress them, and to the cunt which expects so soon to feel their powerful action. Whilst your hand is enjoying itself, and giving your lover the greatest delight also, his hand will be stirring up the very depths of pleasure in you. By the way, before I forget it, let me warn you, when handling a man's prick in this way, do not caress its head too much. It is sensitive, and too much rubbing produces spasms which are very delicious for him, but destructive of your pleasure, for you might make it too excited, and cause him to be too ready to spend. The longer a man takes during the fuck, the greater your pleasure for he does not spend over and over again during a fuck, but once only. That done, he is done too, for the time. So confine your caresses to the shaft of his prick, to his balls, his groin, and his bush, but leave the head of his prick alone, if you are wise. Whilst you are thus caressing him, he will be kissing you. He will be squeezing your dear little bubbies. He will be toying with your tongue with the tip of his. Presently his mouth will kiss you along your neck, until it reaches your bosom. He will kiss your breast with rapture, and nibble each little, hard rosebud. Whilst sending you wild in this manner, his hand will glide over your smooth body and seek your motte; you will feel his hand press between your thighs. Then he will stroke your cunnie so – ," she did it to me, "and he will gently press the lips of your cunt together and tickle your clitoris, this little kind of tongue, a veritable imitation of his own prick, but much smaller; then he will slip his big middle finger deep into your cunnie, and tickle you here."

She slipped hers in and found the narrow, tight inner entrance, which she set on fire immediately with her caressing, making me involuntarily spend.

"You quick little darling!" she exclaimed. "How you do spend! Won't you just like being fucked? Well, now I must not use you up in that way. Keep your spend for when we will have another bout of rub–cunnie. Now, Susan," she continued, again taking possession of my glowing bubbies, "you can feel, even from my poor little feminine hand, how very sensitive your cunt is all about the entrance. It is sensitive all along its whole depth, but the sensitive portion par excellence is about the entrance. The difference between a good fucker and an indifferent one, is in the fact that the really good fucker knows this and does his best to produce the most ecstatic pleasure in you by cultivating this extra sensitivity of the cunnie. Imagine your man now with his two knees between yours. He leans over, but not upon you. He supports himself on his elbow. You take his prick, and plant its head justly and neatly between the lips of your cunnie. Then you put your arms round his waist and, with a little pressure on his part, in goes his prick, quite over the shoulder of its head. Its hood slips back, and you feel the sweet thing filling the outer vestibule of your cunt. Then he draws back until he is almost out, and smoothly and gently pushes in again. This time, with an indescribable thrill, you feel that big head force its way sweetly past the inner, narrow entrance. That thrill is worth a fortune, it is so delicious. Then he draws back until he is almost out; with more decided sweeps he thrusts his powerful swelling prick in, passes the narrows, and buries it halfway in your throbbing and beating cunnie. These movements he continues, always drawing almost out, always gaining, by gentle but smoothly repeated thrusts, ground in your cunt.

"Presently, and all too quickly, you feel his pendant balls touch you beneath your cunnie. Then they beat more firmly against you, and last of all his belly, which has been touching yours all along, presses yours; his hairy motte mingles its brush with yours; your cushion feels his, and his last thrust brings your bodies into the most intimate and close contact. Now the real delight begins. Every stroke, every thrust he gives, is from head to heel of his prick. He gives you long, smooth, deliberate thrusts; every line of those long seven or eight inches tells upon you. You come, you spend, time after time, yet not a drop goes outside. His prick, so to say, closes your cunnie tightly, and your spend only makes its movements more easy inside you. As your pleasure increases, so does his. Presently his agonies of delight begin. All his nerves seem concentrated in the head of his prick, until his sensations are so vivid as almost to take his senses away. Then begin the all too short, as time is concerned, short digs. He shortens his strokes but quickens them, banging his balls against you with great force. Then suddenly he spends, pouring out the fullest riches of his manly strength. You feel it flowing fast into you, like a torrent, like a powerful artery shooting its blood into you. He presses you as though he would crush you into pulp. He forces his prick in, even further than you would think possible. Your downy motte is flattened by his, and all Heaven and its Glories seem open to you! It is over. You have been fucked, and well fucked. Then comes a delightful interval of repose. He lets his body lie all along yours, and he kisses you and pets you and calls you all the pretty things he thinks of. His manly bosom rests on your heaving bubbies, your cunnie, if it has the nutcrackers, tightens and loosens on his prick, giving him further delight. Your motte throbs against his, until you become conscious that his prick does not fill you quite so much as it did, and you feel it gradually slipping out. Your lover gets from between your thighs, and lies on his side, clasping you with his arms, and locking his thighs with yours, as mine do now. The fuck is at an end, and cannot be repeated until his prick stands again."

"What are the nutcrackers, Lucia?" said I gasping for breath. My heart was in my throat with the emotion her description had raised.

"The nutcrackers, darling," said she, "are when your cunnie grasps his prick, as it were, like this," she continued, taking my wrist in her hand, and clasping it at intervals of time with her forefinger and thumb.

"It must be the muscles about the narrow entrance that do it, for my lovers always tell me that they feel the tightening of my cunt about two inches up from their balls, and only there."

"I say, Lucia!"

"What, darling?"

"Do you know by what geographical expression our cunts ought to be called?"

"No. What do you mean?" said Lucia, laughing.

"Why, the Red Sea to be sure! Just inside the lips should be the Gulf of Aden, where it is pretty wide; the narrows should be the Bab-el-Mandeb Straits; and the rest the Red Sea."

"Capital, darling! I'll tell Gladys, who will laugh, I know. Now," she continued, stroking my cunnie in a lively manner, "now, open your thighs again, my own sweetest darling, dear Susan, and let me have you again."

Nothing loth I did so, and soon Lucia was thrilling both herself and me with the pleasure her up and down strokes gave to each of us. At last she made me so tremendously excited that I could lie quiet no longer. I clasped her to my belly with all my might, and as, her cunnie swept down over mine, I gave a vigorous push up with mine. The result was delicious. Both Lucia and I gave vent to a little cry of pleasure, for it so happened that her stiff little clitoris had just reached mine, and my push up made these delicate, charmingly sensitive, little organs penetrate, slightly indeed, but still penetrate, our respective cunnies. The immediate consequence was copious spendings on either side.

Lucia kissed me frantically, gave up the sweeping movement, and pushed her cunt straight at mine. Our clitorises rubbed in a most ravishing manner, as we writhed and thrust, and thrust and writhed, and spent time after time, until fairly exhausted, the perspiration standing in little pearls on our foreheads, we relaxed our hold on one another, and Lucia, resuming her place by my side, lay panting, but quiet.

At length she said, "How Nature does teach, Susan!"

"Yes, dear," said I, still struggling for breath, "but how?"

"But how?" she cried. "Listen to her. But how? Why, what made you give such a delicious buck, darling? It had not entered my head to tell you. I never did it with any girl, myself, and would not have believed it could been of any use had it been proposed. What made you do it?"

"Do you mean why did I push up?"

"Yes, why did you buck, as pushing up is called?"

"Buck rhymes with fuck, does it not, Lucia?"

"Of course, and cunt with hunt, prick with lick, balls with halls, bush with push, and so on, but what has that to do with your bucking, Susan?"

"I can't tell you, darling," said I, kissing her, "I only know I could not lie quiet any longer, and so I gave a buck up, like a horse does when his rider spurs him too much."

"Well, Susan! I can only say that if ever a girl was created for the purpose of fucking, you are she. You seem to take to it like a babe does to its mother's breast. Ah! I do envy the fellows who will have you. I know right well they will think your cunt Heaven."

"I don't know, Lucia! They may not like it at all."

"Oh, won't they?

A man likes a girl to show that he gives her pleasure. They don't like buck-jumping horses, but they do love a good bucking girl, and you do it as if you had been trained to it."

"Well, no one trained me, Lucia, as you know, for I did not imagine any pleasure, such as you have given me, was ever to be extracted from my cunnie. But do you buck when a man is fucking you?"

"Oh yes, but there is an art in it."

"How?"

"Well, you see, the object of bucking is to get in the very last quarter inch of the fellow's prick, which would probably remain outside if you did not buck; to get a good strain onto his balls; to get a good squeeze together of your two mottes. All that adds to the pleasure for both of you. The time to buck is when you feel his balls begin to touch you, then begin a gentle upward stroke, or perhaps a kind of circular stroke, ending with a good bump against his motte. If you begin too soon, you hurry his stroke, a thing to be avoided because you make him spend too soon; the buck should, as I say, be so scientifically done as to complete the entire swallowing up of his prick in your cunnie!"

"I see. Now tell me, Lucia, if I have learnt the lesson right. When a man fucks you, he ought to get his prick in little by little?"

"Just so!"

"Then, after he has once got it in the whole way, he should draw it all but out, and then with one long sweeping stroke, bring it in right up to his balls?"

"Right up to his motte, darling, for his balls touch you first."

" Ah, yes, right up to his motte. Then he should go on so, until he begins to feel that he can no longer withhold his spend, and then he is to fuck like fury."

"Just so – like fury," repeated Lucia, laughing and kissing me.

"Well then! Should I buck like fury too?"

"No, because, unless you kept exact time, you might throw him off his stroke. The best way, then, is to raise your hips as much as possible, and, so to say, give him your cunt more freely than ever. When you feel him spending, clasp your thighs round him. Press him to your bubbies and belly, bite and kiss him, and let him feel that you are as much in heaven as he is."

"Ah, I see!"

"There is another thing you might do which is not bad. When you feel him spending, shake him well, by alternately and quickly drawing up each foot and thrusting it out straight again. Get onto me and I will show you how, darling!"

I got between Lucia's thighs and pressed my cunnie to hers. I could not resist giving her some strokes with mine, so our mutual fury recommenced, but the roles were altered. At first Lucia responded to my thrusts by vigorous pushes; at last she held me tight, so that our cunts exactly covered one another, and our clitorises were side by side, and then, drawing up one knee, she suddenly straightened it again, at the same time drawing up the other and again straightening it. This she continued until we were simply smothered with spend. It was exquisite, for our cunts seemed to open and swallow one another, our clitorises rubbed against one another and when we left off, we found it impossible to lie in such a wet bed. We got up, washed our cunnies, mottes and thighs, and then we walked, naked as we were, to her room, where we got into her cool, clean, dry bed, leaving mine to dry as best it could.

Then Lucia said, "Susan, darling! There is only one serious drawback to fucking, and that is its extreme danger!"

"Danger?" I echoed. "What danger, Lucia?"

"Babies!" she said.

"Babies!"

"Yes, babies! You see, darling, when a man spends in us, he shoots into us enough stuff to make thousands of babies if, like fishes, we were capable of producing thousands of eggs at one time."

"Eggs! Lucia! What are you talking of?"

"Facts, Susan! Solid, sober facts, of which I must tell you too, and which you must remember, and be well on your guard always."

"Oh, Lucia!" I cried. "Is that really true? Don't humbug me, darling! If there is one thing I have longed to know about, it is how babies are born. I, of course, could not be so entirely ignorant, but that I knew that a baby proceeds from its mother. The Bible tells us that much. I guessed, too, that something mysterious happened between husband and wife whereby a baby was manufactured, but I had really no idea of fucking! I had no idea that my cunnie was anything more than an accident of nature. The truth is that since you have taught me these exquisite pleasures, the real facts have begun to dawn upon me; but even now I am ignorant of why fucking should produce babies, and you astonish me still more by speaking of eggs! Are women hens, then? When do they lay eggs? Tell me! I am dying to know, if only from a scientific point of view. Tell me, darling!" and I kissed Lucia again and again, as if to coax her to tell me a secret she was really quite as anxious to impart to me as I was to hear it; only, in my eagerness, I forgot that one who had been so free from all restraint, both of action and word, with me would not be like my mother, who used to tell me I was too young to understand whenever I approached her as to this thorny, or perhaps I might more appropriately say this "prickly" subject of creation.

Lucia laughed at my eagerness.

" Ah, Susan!" she cried, clasping me in her arms, and kissing me so kindly. "I can see that it is more from a desire to learn the matter as a science, than to know how to protect your sweet little belly from swelling, that you are so eager about it. Well, darling; though my most particular desire is to teach you how to defend yourself from the deadly effects of an unprotected fuck, however nice it may be at the time, yet, as you wish it, I will give you the history of your womb and ovaries, of what they produce; and of the spend of a man, and what it produces, scientifically, as a doctor, for I know the subject well, having often and often talked it over with doctors, fucking friends and lovers of mine. Don't interrupt me more than you can help, and I will tell you exactly, point by point, what the process is. You know already in theory, and soon, I hope, will know it also by practice, what fucking is – that sweetest, most ravishing of all delights. Fucking is only a means to an end. The real end, in nature, is procreation. Fucking causes the male to part with his fertilising spend. It is wrong to call it "seed," for the seed is really in the woman, not in the man. The man fertilises it, just as your bees and insects fertilise flowers by shaking the pollen onto the stamens. In every flower there is a cunt, darling."

"A cunt!" I cried.

"Yes, dearest, a regular, sweet-smelling, beautiful cunt. But most plants have hermaphrodite flowers i.e., blossoms which contain both the male and the female organs of reproduction. Of these plants, some, however, have male flowers and female flowers quite separate from one another. The bees and other insects go from flower to flower. They accidentally gather pollen from one, and carry it to another. Some of the pollen shakes off them onto the stamens of the second flower, the impregnation takes place the flower,the pretty cunt withers and the petals fall off, but the seed swells, ripens and in time is fit for sowing again."

"But surely a girl's cunt does not wither like that, Lucia?"

"No, darling," she said, laughing and stroking mine with her slender fingers."

"Our cunts don't wither, but they certainly are not improved by child bearing. They lose their freshness, and when you consider how much, how greatly they must be expanded by a child, however small, being forced into the world through them, you can imagine such a thing happening as permanent enlargement. But any increase in size – i.e., diameter – materially affects the pleasure of subsequent fucks, and I know that men complain of this enlargement of their wives' cunts. Some get bigger than others; but undoubtedly the best fucks are given by cunts which have never granted the passage of a child into the world. However, I am digressing."

"Oh, not at all, Lucia! This is most interesting. To think that a rose, for instance, is only another form of a cunt! Oh, fancy talking of a nosegay as a bunch of cunts!" And I laughed.

"Just so! It is quite true, Susan, and when a gentleman gives you a moss-rose, it is a very direct allusion to your cunt, darling. The flower is the cunt, the moss the bush which grows about it. So if you wore a moss-rose in your bosom, and gave it to a gentleman who is up to sniff, he will at once remember the sweet little mossy cunt, which lies so snug and warm between your lovely thighs."

"Ah, that is the language of flowers. I see it. Now I know why a moss-rose means love."

"Just so. Because a woman surrenders her cunt as the gift of love to the man she loves. But we are far from our point, Susan. Let us return to our subject. Men have a pair of balls, as you now know. From these balls proceeds, by a roundabout road, the so-called seed, which, deposited in our cunts, produces babies. But we girls, too, have a pair of balls."

"Balls! Girls have balls, Lucia?"

"Yes, darling, but inside, deep, somewhere near the backbone. These balls are called ovaries. Once a month a ripe girl has a flow of blood, as it were. It is at this time she is producing eggs."

"Eggs!"

"Yes, eggs, that are very small indeed, not bigger than a pin's head, but real eggs all the same. There is a tube leading from each ovary to the top of the womb, and down these tubes the eggs travel. It is still a question whether the eggs reach the womb fertilised, or whether they are fertilised in the womb, but that is a question for science to unravel. Our question is, how to prevent them being fertilised? Well, now listen. The womb is an organ about the size of a medium pear. It is pear-shaped. Its broadest part is highest, the stalk end, as it were, which enters our cunts, or vaginas, as doctors call them, at the top. Here there is a small hole in the communication between the womb and the cunt. This hole is very tightly closed, but tight as it is, it can allow the spermatozoids to pass, and there are little filaments, like hairs, extremely small indeed, lining this hole, which continually work, sucking up all they can get to come from the cunt. Well, a man's spend literally swarms with spermatozoids. Hush! I'll tell you what they are, but give me time. They are little microscopic objects, something like tadpoles in shape, having a head and a long tail. They swim, and dart and wriggle about. When a man spends in us, he shoots hundreds of thousands in, which at once dart about in a perfect lake of our spend, corked up in our cunts by the man's big prick. Of course, if the mouth of the womb be left unprotected, all the little reptiles have to do is to walk up the hole and get into the womb, helped by the cilix, which I have spoken of as like little hairs. Even if they don't do it at once, they, or some of them, will remain clinging to the lining of our cunts, and in time they will make for the mouth of the womb and get in. Then somewhere or other, they will meet with our egg, if one is ready. They stick their heads into it, and the mischief is done. The egg is fertilised, and in nine months' time the result will be a fat baby."

"How wonderful! Lucia, you darling! You can't tell how glad, how delighted I am to learn this. Now I understand why what Martha calls love children come into the world. I thought that only married women could have babies, yet I knew that some unmarried girls had some too, and I wondered how they got them, as they had no husbands. I can't tell you all the absurd ideas I used to have on this subject. I wish I had a book to read all about it in, with pictures, so that I might be sure I thoroughly understood it all. It would give me great delight. And to think of those marvellous tadpole things! I suppose, then, that the reason some women never have families must be either because their husband shoots no tadpoles into them, or they have no eggs ready?"

"Ah, Susan! That is a subject of which I am ignorant, and I don't think doctors even are agreed about it. But I can only tell you that I would never trust to luck, and go without protection from probable evil results, when I have a man. As to eggs not being ready, why, the worst is that these horrible little tadpoles only ask for a snug, warm, moist place to live in, and there they will remain alive; so that, as the egg is bound to come sooner or later in a healthy woman, the tadpole is equally bound to get at it. Say that one of my lovers was here now, and first fucked me, and then fucked you, first one each: it is now ten or twelve days since I had my monthlies – when did you last have yours?"

"Last week, darling."

"Very well. You would almost certainly have a baby this day in nine months. I might escape but only if the tadpoles in me all perish from perhaps want of some ailment, which a man has, but I have not. But if a tadpole, one only, happened to live until I was next ill, I too should have a baby, a few days after yours. Oh, fucking is heavenly; but it is terribly dangerous when the wedding ring does not make it the right thing in the eyes of the world."

"But, Lucia," I said, an uneasy feeling coming over me, making all the life seem to leave my hitherto hot little cunt, "if fucking be so terribly dangerous, how is it you care to run such fearful risks? I should imagine that fear would take almost all the sense of pleasure away. I know I should think of nothing but the tadpoles. I don't think I will let any man fuck me, now I have heard what you have told me."

"Oh dear, yes, you will, Susan," cried Lucia, laughing. "I am glad I have scared you so well, because you must always bear in mind what I have told you, that, unless you are fully protected, you can't have a more dangerous thing in you than a man's prick."

"But how do you get this protection, Lucia?" I asked anxiously. "And how have you escaped? To hear you, one would imagine that you do hardly anything else than fuck, and you appear to have a perfect armoury of pricks and balls at your disposal."

"So I have, darling," said Lucia, kissing me and reviving my crestfallen cunnie with her soothing hand. "I should have to reckon all my lovers, and it would take more than the fingers on your two hands and the toes on your feet, and mine too, to be able to count all the darling pricks that have been up my cunnie, and as to the number of times they have given me the full delight, I really could not, at the moment, tell you, though I have all recorded at home, names, dates, numbers of fucks and all. But then I protected myself. It is extremely easy"

"But how? But how?" I cried.

"Well, all one has to do is to prevent the tadpoles from getting into our womb, and that can be easily done by means of a piece of sponge."

"Sponge!"

"Yes, sponge! Look, I will show you, and she jumped out of bed, her lovely white nakedness shining in the light of the candles as she walked to her chest of drawers. She took a little ivory box off it and returned towards me.

How lovely she looked. Her elegant figure, her round, polished shoulders, her beautiful limbs, her broad, gracefully-shaped hips, and the brilliant whiteness of her belly and thighs brought out vividly by the rich, dark, thick bush which covered her swelling motte, whilst her exquisite, rosy-tipped bubbies stood out firm, like those of a statue in marble; these all flashed on me, and were all enhanced by the natural elegance of her movements. Oh! I felt that were I a man, I should forget all about possible danger to her, and should desire of all things to clasp that lovely body to mine, and thrust my fervent, burning prick in, up to my balls, in the sweet little cunt I could see half hidden under the dark brown hair, in its snug retreat between her beautiful thighs. Should I then, when naked before a man equally naked, forget my danger in his manly beauty? Suppose, instead of being a girl, Lucia had been a handsome youth? Suppose, instead of that lovely, pouting little cunt before my eyes, I saw a pair of splendid balls, surmounted by a magnificent big, big, big prick, all stiff and standing, such as she had described, would I not be very likely to forget that all that splendour covered a deep danger? That those glorious pendants might originate irretrievable disaster, and that prick, so handsome, so alluring, so desire–compelling, might leave behind it unutterable woe, if I admitted it within my burning and randy little cunt. I felt grateful then to Lucia, that before any such terrible temptations to indulge my passions were likely to assail me, she had opened my eyes to the sense of danger, but I resolved to do as she said and to indulge myself, so soon as I found the lover, and so soon as I quite knew all about the protection, of which she had so eloquently praised the merits. These thoughts flashed through me in a much, much shorter time than it has taken me to jot them down, sweet girl-reader. Ah, dear girls, read these pages attentively, and profit by the experience you will gain. Then lie with your lover, then fuck with your lover, gain all the pleasures, and avoid all the dangers of fruitful, delicious love!

Lucia sat on the bed, and unscrewing the top of the ivory box, drew out of it a fat, little glass bottle, having a wide mouth securely fastened with a ground glass-stopper. Putting in her tapering finger, she fished up a little ivory bar, in the centre of which was fastened a rose-coloured silken thread. This she pulled out until it lifted up a sponge of very fine texture, about as big as a large walnut. The sponge was full of moisture, which she squeezed out into the bottle, and then she held it out to me.

"See!" she said. "This sponge, Susan, is my shield and buckler! When I am going to fuck, I first put it into my cunnie, so," doing it as she spoke, "I push it in with my finger as far as I can, and my lover rams it home with his stiff prick When it is home it covers the mouth of my womb, and when my lover spends, it comes between my womb and his prick. No spend can possibly pass through it, and even if any did, the tadpoles would be all killed by the liquid with which this sponge is filled. It is a mixture of carbonised oil, glycerine and a little rose water to give it a pleasant smell. The carbonic acid, small though it be in quantity, is sufficient for the purpose, and no tadpole can stand its effects. Well, this little piece of ivory prevents the up–and–down movements of my lover's prick from rucking up the cord, and pushing it, too, up to the top of my cunnie; and after every fuck I make it the practice, not only to pull out the sponge, which of course brings out most of my lover's spend, and mine too with it, but I syringe my cunnie well with a mixture of the same lotion as was in the sponge and soft, warm water. Every atom of spend must thus be removed, and I can't possibly run any danger. The syringing if done soon enough, would do equally well; but then goodbye to the delicious, quiet lying with the sweet prick in me, because, my womb being unprotected, a tadpole might, even in that short time, get in! Also goodbye to alfresco fucks, in the green fields, or in the train, or in a drawing–room, or anywhere where it would be impossible to use a syringe; unless, indeed, my lover had any letters about him. But I don't like letters. I like a naked prick. I always fancy I feel the dead skin of the letter when my lovers use them."

"What do you mean by letters, Lucia?"

"Oh! they are not real letters. I do not know why they are so called, Susan; but they are little coverings of skin, or thin india rubber, which men put on their pricks, and which either fit them tight, being elastic, or are tied close to their balls with little ribbons. Then, of course, not a drop of spend can get into me, because it is all caught by the letter."

"But that seems very convenient."

"Well, it is! but I prefer my sponge, which is quite as safe, and does not interpose itself between my lover's prick and the lining of my cunt."

"And what is the syringe like, Lucia? Is it like those that gardeners use?"

"Bless you, no, girl! It is – but I have one! Ah, happy thought, I have some warm water here; we will syringe our cunts out now! Jump up, dear!"

I did so. Lucia put the basin on the floor, and getting a tumbler, she filled it with warm water. Then she got a long box, about eight inches long, by two wide, and two deep. Out of this she took a long, flexible tube, about eighteen inches long, with an ivory nozzle, and also, in the middle, a kind of large bellows swelling. To the ivory nozzle she fixed another slightly curved, but rigid tube, rounded at the end and pierced there with holes. This passed through a piece of polished ebony, or stiff leather, shaped like an oval, and big enough to quite cover a cunt, which indeed was the object of it. Seating herself over the basin, she put one end of the tube into the tumbler of water, whilst she passed the rigid end right up her cunnie, until the shield came over its lips: holding the shield tightly against her cunt, she began to squeeze the bulb in the centre of the flexible tube, and soon I saw that the water in the tumbler was diminishing rapidly in quantity.

"Are you pumping that water into your cunt, Lucia?" I asked.

"Yes, darling, and it fills it deliciously."

"There!" she said, relaxing her pressure on the shield, upon which the water rushed out of her cunt into the basin with a splash, "there! that was very refreshing! Come, and let me syringe you, darling!"

"But," said I, "perhaps that won't go up me, Lucia! Remember I have still my maidenhead! No lover has cleared that obstacle away in me, as yours have in you."

"Oh, that won't matter. You would have to have a very, very fine maidenhead to prevent this passing, and, as a matter of fact, I have felt my finger go past it."

She caught me round the waist, and put her middle finger up my cunt as she spoke, until her knuckles touched its lips.

"There! I can feel your maidenhead plainly, Susan. The tip of my finger is a good inch past it. Don't you feel me pressing at it?"

"I do," said I.

After this I made no further objection. The tube gave me a delightful sensation as it passed up. I held the shield firmly pressed against me. Lucia renewed the water, and worked the syringe. It was delicious! The water quite filled me inside and I had a kind of foretaste of what it must feel like when one's cunt is filled by a fine, voluminous prick!

Having dried our mottes, Lucia put away her syringe and sponge, and then we returned to bed, but she asked me to let her have a good long look at my cunnie, which, she said, was such a perfect jewel she wished to examine it thoroughly. To be able to do this with ease, she asked me to lie down on my back, across the bed, so that my legs might hang down over the side. I did so. Then, she fell to admiring my feet, ankles, calves, knees and thighs, kissing them all, as her wanton eyes wandered to regions higher still. It was exquisite, all these warm and almost passionate kisses!

"Now, Susan, darling! Put one leg over each of my shoulders. Ah, that is it. Now I have this sweet little cunt of yours in full view! Lie still, darling, whilst I examine it to my entire satisfaction, in all its beautiful details! "

I lay quiet as a mouse. I felt her arms encircle my thighs, and her hands approach my motte, the long, curling bush of which she stroked, and then her fingers, separating and parting the hairs which crossed the soft entrance to my cunnie. These delicate little touches gave me infinite pleasure. It seemed as though Lucia delighted in giving me fresh and fresher experience. Presently I felt her press her thumbs gently so as to open the top of my cunt.

"Oh! the sweet, sweet, little ruby clitoris!" she cried, "Oh, Susan, you have such a pretty, pretty little tongue here. I really must kiss it!" and down went her hot lips onto my cunt.

I cried out, "Ah! Lucia! Don't do that, darling. That is not nice."

"Not nice!" cried she, raising her head. "Do you mean, Susan dearest, that I hurt you; that my kisses there are unpleasant to you?"

"No, darling, but surely it is not a nice thing to put one's lips on such a part of the body as that."

"Oh!" said she. "Is that all? Now, darling, I like to do it to you, and I like it done to myself, and I strongly suspect when you have had a little more of it you will like it extremely. Just see if you don't!"

Down went her lascivious mouth onto my cunt again. Really and truly I had liked it there the moment I felt what the sensation was like. I had only cried out because I felt the small stock of modesty I had left repugnant to such an action. However, as Lucia said she liked doing it, I did not mind, and I lay still.

But only for a moment, for Lucia, having seized my stiff little clitoris between her lips, began to mouth it, and to touch it smartly with her tongue in so ravishing a manner that I could not help crying out with the excessive pleasure she gave me. I did not resist, but I could not lie still. I moved under her devouring mouth, driven half frantic with the powerful sensations of exquisite, almost painful delight she gave me. Lucia seemed prepared for this, for she followed all my movements with skill and patience. If I snatched her electrified prey from between her lips, she instantly seized it again whilst her fingers tickled my motte or groin, or gently plucked at my curling bush. Presently she left my clitoris and ran on the line of my cunt with the tip of her tongue. I felt her face press my motte, her hands smoothly passing over my belly until they reached my bubbies. They took possession of them; my nipples were sweetly squeezed between her fingers, whilst she felt my breasts and magnetised them with her caressing palms. Her cheeks felt so hot against my thighs that they seemed to burn them. But oh, how to express my astonished sensations when I distinctly felt her tongue, gathered as it were into a rod, penetrate deep within my cunnie's lips, and touch the exquisitely sensitive Straits of Bab-el-Mandeb.

"Lucia! Lucia! For God's sake, don't do it any more. You are killing me with pleasure. Oh, dear girl, if you don't take care! I'm going to spend! I'm go... ing to spend! To spend I tell you! Oh... h... h... h... h!" and I felt a flood leave me. It must have inundated Lucia's face, but she only continued her actions, until at last, having spent several times, I actually managed, by drawing my foot up and planting my toes on a delicious, elastic breast, to push her away.

Like a tigress bereft of her prey, Lucia rose, with fire flashing from her eyes, her cheeks red with passion, her bosom shining from the moist offerings I had ejected, and seizing me by the thighs she placed me full length on the bed, and then sprang on top of me. With her knees she opened mine and forcibly spread out my thighs, and then commenced a passionate, amorous combat, for which, in truth, I was nothing loth. Our cunts seemed to fit, and our clitorises clashed, seeming to penetrate deeper than they had yet done. Our mottes got drenched with our mutual spend. I twisted, I wriggled, I fought valiantly, and played my part to perfection, for I was maddened with the almost supernatural excess of voluptuous feelings this lovely burning Sappho inspired me with.

At length, after a struggle prolonged until nature seemed to become exhausted, Lucia lay motionless but panting on my belly, until we had both somewhat recovered our lost breath. Then, still lying between my thighs, Lucia raised her head, and looked inexpressible love, and kissing me with rapture, gently rubbing her bubbies crossways with mine, she said,

"There, Susan! I have no more to teach you of the pleasure one girl can take with another. Some women even prefer such delights to those which man can give them. I don't share their opinions, but after you have learnt what it is to be well fucked you must tell me."

"Oh, Lucia, I can't tell! Perhaps I may after all find a sweet cunt like yours better even than a fine prick."

"Well! I don't think so," said she, laughing. "But it is getting late, my pet. Come, let us go to your room. Your bed is probably dry by now, and mine, look at it! Swamped!"

And so it was. We rose, washed our cunts and bushes and thighs once more, and went to my room. Our modest chemises once again disappeared from sight under our nightdresses, through which the little hills of our bosoms made themselves very apparent, and then we got into my bed, and locking one another in our arms we soon fell fast asleep.

I dare say my reader will say that it was wonderful how an innocent girl like myself could have been so quickly converted into a perfect Lesbian. But, dear reader, if of the male sex, do you remember how quickly you learnt to love when the fair woman who first taught you what your prick was for, took it and pressed it in the velvet palms of her hands? After that first powerful appeal to your passions, how long did ignorance prevail over knowledge? Did you remain shy and coy, or did you plunge at once into that delightful vortex of voluptuous passion? I know your reply; you need not answer. And you, oh, sweet girl, when your eager lover first passed a passionate hand under your petticoats and, seizing the lovely prey of your ardent little cunt, glided a tempting finger into its hot depths, did not that sweet cunt beg you to listen to his prayers, and having once been ravished of your modest maidenhead, and having felt the rapture of that stalwart prick, the soft pressure of those pleasant feeling balls, and the inexpressible poesy of the movements of the blissful fuck, tell me, did you hesitate to open your thighs a second, a third, nay, a thousandth time to your nasty lover? Ce n'est que le premier pas qui coute, after that the progress is rapid. Once the spark has been set to the combustibles, the fire rages. So it was with me. Lucia had suddenly attacked me by the weakest side; without knowing or thinking I yielded, and my readers will see if I have ever had reason to regret commencing a course of pleasure which has made my life up to this time one continual feast, one endless song of happy delight.

CHAPTER IV
THE TADPOLES, ETC.

We slept long and soundly after our exploits of the night, and it was already near noon before either of us awoke. Lucia cried out when, on looking at my watch, she saw what the time was, and without waiting to give me any more caresses, she fled to her room, bidding me at the same time to be quick with my toilet.

On going downstairs Martha met me in the breakfast room, and looked all astonishment.

"My goodness, child," said she, "whatever makes you so late this morning? I went to see why you were not up. It gave me quite a turn when you did not come down at your usual hour. I could not but think of your poor, dear papa, who died in his sleep. But when I saw you and Miss Lucia sleeping so calmly in one another's arms, and saw by your bosoms rising and falling that it was only natural sleep, I left off being frightened. Ah, you did look a pretty pair. I could have wished, though, instead of Miss Lucia, I had seen a handsome young husband in your bed, who on waking would have given his pretty bird a sweet wakening, as young, active husbands always wake their wives."

As she was saying these last few words Lucia came into the room.

"What was that you were saying, Mrs. Warmart, about young husbands waking their wives?" said she.

"I was just telling Miss Susan how I wished you had been her young man, Miss, when I saw the two of you so fast asleep this morning when I went to call her, and I was a–saying that if you had been, you would have waked her in a way she would have dearly liked."

"Ah, true enough. So I would, and I can tell you, Mrs. Warmart, that when I saw how nicely Susan is made, I wished I was a young man myself last night, twenty times."

"Ah, well, young ladies!" replied Martha, laughing, but still sufficiently seriously. "You must not let your imaginations run away too much with you. Young men are not to be trusted, remember, and temptation comes very often when one is least on one's guard, and what is pleasure at first often ends in pain at last."

"Yes, Mrs. Warmart, that I believe is true enough! But now have you any breakfast for us? I am hungry enough to feel that I could gobble up Susan, and if I let my hunger get the better of me I would make a complete end of her, which is more than the young man would do."

Martha laughed and quickly put our breakfast on the table. Lucia and I, famished with our long fast, gladly fell to, and we both ate heartily.

Ah, now I feel better, Susan. How do you feel this morning? None the worse, I hope, for our delicious *tête-à-tête* last night?"

"All the better, I think," said I, "only I feel rather stretched in the thigh joints."

"So do I," said Lucia, "now that comes from want of practice. It is such an age since I opened my thighs to anyone!

"However," she continued, "it won't be long, I hope, before I shall have lots more practice that way; and my lovely Susan shall begin hers. Oh, Susan! How I almost envy you, to know for the first time what a man is."

I laughed.

"Look, darling!" Lucia ran on, "I want to write a letter to Gladys, and to do one or two little things for myself, so I'll just run up to my room. You won't mind my leaving you for a little while, will you?"

"No, dear!" I said, "I will go and feed my little pets and gather some flowers..."

"And dream of young men!" laughed Lucia.

"Very likely," said I, "especially when I have gathered a bunch of cunts."

"You darling!" exclaimed Lucia, kissing me in her boisterous manner, "You deserve a most luscious fucking, you come so quick in mind and body," and pressing me once more in her arms, and kissing me again, she ran off.

Often and often have I wondered how I never seemed to see an inkling of that hell which I have so often read of as being the immediate result of following the natural bent of one's desires. I so often read, and have so often heard good people say, that the inevitable result of 'sinning' (and in the eyes of 999 out of 1,000 good women, fucking with anyone not one's husband is sin – hardly anything else being so) was miserable repentance, and a wretched state of one's conscience.

With me it has been just the reverse. I admit I have been fortunate, in so far as my acts have not been productive of unhappy results. I have no doubt we all regret having done anything which produces unfortunate consequences either for ourselves or for others, but such acts may not necessarily be sins. I don't know that a married woman enjoys her husband any the more because what he does to her in bed is 'lawful and right'. I fancy a prick is a prick, and a cunt a cunt, whether the conjunction of them be 'lawful' or 'unlawful'. All I know is, that whether the prick be that of a married or of an unmarried man, it makes no difference to me, so long as it be a good one, and well wielded. My cunt seems naturally formed to receive pricks, and all I can say is that those men who are gentle in idea and behaviour are ever welcome to it, and afford it and me such pleasure that I never say no unless prudential reasons cause me, with a sigh, to decline the delightful offering.

I don't know what the current of my thoughts was that morning, but I imagine I was looking forward to those halcyon days when, according to Lucia, I should have the voluptuous delight of knowing, from vivid experience, what it felt like to have a handsome and vigorous man stretched at full length between my glowing thighs, delighting me with his caresses!

When I came in an hour later, Lucia was still upstairs, and I sat down with a book in my hand, but my mind was still running on the pleasures I had so lately learnt.

After a while Lucia came downstairs, dressed ready for a walk, and holding a sketching block in her hand.

"Come, Susan dear," she said, "we breakfasted so late that I think neither of us could eat any lunch. Let us go out for a ramble over the fields. We will take some biscuits in our pockets, and I may show you some sketches I made. Perhaps if I can find a pretty view I may make a sketch this afternoon."

"All right, Lucia!" I cried, and running upstairs, I quickly put on my hat and light jacket, and joined Lucia down in the breakfast room.

We sallied forth, having first told Mrs. Warmart we might not be in again for some hours.

"Ah, that's right, Miss Lucia!" said the old dame, looking at my sweet cousin with beaming face and smiles. "You are the right sort! I do believe that if you had not come here, poor Miss Susan would be sitting indoors now, moping to death.

"Susan," said Lucia, as we made our way along the path, "do you know one of the things you should carefully cultivate is exercise, good outdoor exercise, and walking is one of the best, because it is the least fatiguing, whilst at the same time it calls into play every muscle of your body. A good walker always carries himself upright: he gets good, square shoulders, and a fine, projecting chest, and he is always in good trim. It adds firmness to the flesh, and tone to the body, and a girl who wishes to preserve a good figure, to have firm breasts, firm, round and delightful to see and feel, can't do better than take plenty of walking exercise, in the fields if possible. Besides the mere healthiness of the walk, there is another and not unimportant reason. Now although, as I explained last night, the sponge and syringe are perfect safeguards against the insidious approach to our wombs of the active spermatozoa, yet, if it be possible to still further defend ourselves, we should be foolish not to do it. Now, without being in the least degree uncharitable towards my neighbours, who in public denounce what they call illicit intercourse with men as sinful and wicked, yet my own experience has shown me that a very great number of ladies, both married and unmarried, have their lovers, whilst I know that numbers of shop girls and servant maids have theirs also, and I do not think I am at all overshooting the mark when I say that at least one half of those shop girls and servant maids have their lovers at least once a week, if not more often.

"But, as hardly any of them use any precaution whatever, it should follow that half the nubile women should, whether married or not, be always in the family way, whereas the truth is that this is not so, and why? Well, most of the girls of whom I speak are obliged to have their fucks either in the fields, or in some hidden corner, not in bed, and so soon as Master Johnnie Prick is out of their cunnies, the girls spring to their feet so as not to attract attention should any chance passenger come by.

"The consequence is that the seed has a tendency to run out of their little cunts. This I believe to be the reason why servants and shop girls so frequently escape being impregnated.

"But take young, married couples. Now I think you may be sure that during the honeymoon fucking is the constant action which goes on. By rights, then, every young, married woman should have a baby in nine months from the time she first went to bed with her husband. The facts however are against this theory. It is so comparatively rare for a baby to appear so punctually that when one does keep such excellent time, the husband gets clapped on the back, as if he must be a splendid performer, a perfect stallion, a grand bull, whereas, if the truth were known, his wife is rather a lazy young person, who prefers lying on the sofa to going out for a walk! By and by, you will, when in society, have opportunities of observing the truth of what I say viz – that the active young wives who walk are much longer free from pregnancy than those who do not walk, and that the worst thing a girl who wishes to become a mother can do, is to be active on her feet, or on horseback! Consequently, girls who, like myself, have no right husbands, but dozens of ardent, strong-backed lovers, can't do better than take plenty of exercise, either on foot or on horseback, as it is an additional safeguard from having a swelling and inconvenient belly!"

I listened quietly to those words of wisdom, and I strongly recommend my dear girl readers to mark them too, and to put in practice the sound advice of my dear cousin Lucia. For, however delightful fucking may be, there are people who could not stand in the light of day if the results are to be an increase of the population, and you, dear unmarried girls, are of that number.

Having at length arrived in a field of several acres' extent, with high hedges all round and trees dotted here and there, Lucia said she thought we might rest under one of the trees, and she would show me her sketches.

She chose a spot some distance from the path, and the moment she produced her watercolour drawings from the pocket of her sketch block, I saw why she had gone so far from where any chance passer-by might see her pretty pictures, or hear our conversation! My breath was almost taken away when the first she put into my hand represented a fine and handsome young man, perfectly naked!

Everything was there! The picture was perfect! It was beautifully done, and was a portrait. I could recognise the features of the handsome, manly face of my cousin Charlie Althair; but I did not scan those features so eagerly as I did certain others, halfway between his chin and his feet. For there I saw most beautifully delineated the charms, the charms, which affect a woman most powerfully. The moment Lucia had chosen to represent, was when Charlie was not in that state in which his lady-loves most liked to find him; in other words, he was in a state of complete repose. Lucia had drawn his bush perfectly, and out of the lower portion of it grew that sweet, sweet chubby prick, reposing on a pair of well rounded, tightly closed-up balls.

I could see at once that it was an exact representation, though I had never seen the real object of which I had the portrait before me. I felt my cheeks crimson, and my stays grew so tight on my bosom that I felt like choking.

Lucia said nothing. She very quietly watched my increasing agitation until I turned my burning eyes on her face.

"Well, Susan! That is Charlie Althair, in puris naturalibus! What do you think of him?"

"Oh, Lucia! And did you do this yourself?"

"Yes, dear. But it was difficult enough to get Charlie as quiet as that," and she laid the point of her pretty finger on his prick. "That article, when I am near, is generally in this condition," and she slid another sketch over the first one in my hands.

"Oh! My!" On gazing on this second work of undoubted art and skill I could not resist giving vent to a cry of admiration and wonder. For there, in all its glorious might, power and beauty, was what I presumed was the same prick, but erect, grand, swollen, big and certainly as still as if carved out of living flesh-coloured marble. Its curious, wonderful-looking head was uncovered, and for the first time I quite understood the vivid description Lucia had given me of this beautiful member the night before. How I studied it! How my cunt burnt and throbbed at the sight! I could feel my breasts swell, their nipples grow hard and my clitoris stand. I was forced to put my hand between my thighs, and Lucia, delighted, gently pushed me on my back, and looking carefully round to be sure no uncalled-for intruder was near, she quickly slipped her hand under my petticoats, found my beating cunnie, and gently insinuated a spend-provoking, but most grateful finger deep between its burning lips.

Whilst she thus imitated the movements, I held before me the delicious object her pleasant finger represented to me very palpably. Oh, let the day soon come when, instead of a girl's finger, this glorious prick might invade my longing cunt, and I might feel on my rounded haunches the weight of those splendid balls. I could have lain so for an indefinite time, but Lucia, always careful, said the place was too open, and that such exquisite sports were better deferred until we could safely indulge in them where, by no possibility, prying eyes might see us at play. Reluctantly I resumed my sitting position, and Lucia replaced my petticoats, but my faithful Spot came sniffing, and Lucia laughingly lifted my dress for him, saying that no doubt his tongue would be as clever as her finger. Good, dear Spot. The first male being that ever kissed my cunnie. How grateful to your loving mistress was your soft, hot tongue that afternoon! Picture after picture did Lucia show me, most of them illustrative of amorous couples indulging in the joy of erotic bliss. Drawn by the hand of one who fully sympathised with all she had delineated, and by a hand evidently possessing marvellous skill and dexterity, these pictures were really gems of art.

Nothing could more powerfully appeal to the passions than these lovely, living representations did, and had Lucia doubted my perfect willingness to embark on a career of Paphian exploits, she could not have possibly hit upon a better method for convincing a hesitating mind. My mind, however, required no further encouragement than it had already received from her words. These voluptuous actions, transferred in all their naked beauty to the papers I held in my hands, only tended to increase the eager desire I had to take my part in the most delicious and exhilarating of all pursuits. Again and again I looked them over, and begged for more and more, until Lucia wisely said that my colour was so like that of a peony, we must really continue our walk, until my cheeks had resumed the natural rosy tints which usually adorned them. So Spot was relieved of a duty, he had apparently relished, and one he had performed marvellously well, for though I had spent perfect floods the faithful dog had allowed none to run to waste.

"Oh, Lucia!" I said, as we continued our walk, "when shall I be able to go with you to Sunninghill? For I am to go with you, darling, am I not? You would not leave me here to mope after you had gone?"

"Of course you shall come with me, darling Susan I!" she cried. "But so much depends upon old Penwick. I think we must hurry the old gentleman up. We will go and see him in his office tomorrow when we go to Worcester."

"And does Gladys know I am coming with you, darling, dearest Lucia?"

"Oh yes. But until she gets my letter, which I sent to post this morning, she won't know that our snug Nunnery is to have another lovely novice. We won't go to Sunninghill, Susan! We shall go to London, where I am badly wanted. Read this," and she gave me a letter, evidently written by a lady from the character of the writing. It ran thus:

Dearest Lucia,

When are you coming back? When will you be able to leave our little country cousin, and return to the disconsolate swains who, poor fellows, we are obliged to tell that they cannot be accommodated because our loveliest girl is away? I hope you are not playing fox, and that all this while you are enjoying the pleasures of love with foxhunting squires, grave country curates, or handsome young farmers. What is Susan like? Has she any penchant for our naughty ways? Have you sounded her? Do you think, supposing she is pretty enough – and she should be, as she is of our same blood, a blood which has never produced an ugly child yet – she could be induced to give up her chance of a single husband for the certainty of a plurality of much more interesting and ever fresh lovers? To be plain, do you think she will fuck, if the chance be offered her of doing so without fear of evil consequences? Of course, unless she is naturally inclined to do so, I don't advocate her coming as a nun, and just now it would be awkward to have her as a guest, for never have I known so busy a season. Our guests are numerous, and not a bed unoccupied from one end of the week to the other. If those beds could speak they would tell us some pretty stories. I believe adultery is greatly on the increase, and some of our ladies have more than one lover apiece. Poor Annette and I are, however, really to be either greatly pitied or immensely envied. I don't know which, for sometimes I feel as if my back were broken, I get such a lot of it.

Not one single night for the last three weeks in bed alone, and a fresh man every night, not the same man twice in a week. It is the same with Annette.

My usual time will be next week, and there will be only Annette. So do, for goodness sake, come, if only to pay a flying visit, but come and relieve us for that week, otherwise I fear our disappointed lovers may fly to fields not so wholesome as ours. Bring your own dear little cunt to the rescue, and if possible bring Susan's also.

Charlie Althair says he has not had a real good night since he last had you. I believe he has adorned his prick with one or two more maidenheads whilst you were away. He loves tender virgins, and makes them love him!

Adieu, darling Lucia. I am to have Sir Thomas Gordon tonight. You may remember I had him about eighteen months ago at his mother's house.

Your poor loving cousin,
GLADYS

"Well," said Lucia as I handed back the letter, "what do you think I told Gladys in my reply this morning?"

"I suppose you said that you thought I would go with you, dear."

"Yes, indeed, I did. And I said more! I told her that you were absolutely beautiful from the crown of your head to the soles of your feet, and that your disposition was so amorous, your temperament so ardent, that you would be the very finest possible acquisition. I told her that I had found you, darling, in a state of extraordinary simplicity and ignorance, but that the moment I reflected from the mirror of my mind and my experience the ways of enlightening knowledge, you had spread out not only your lovely, rounded bosom, but your exquisitely chiselled thighs to receive all I had to give you. I said that so plentiful was the will of love, between the aforesaid voluptuous thighs, that it hardly asked to be touched before it overflowed with the offerings of sympathy, and that though the sweet cunnie sheltered by its lovely bush, and was virgin of virgin, yet I knew that, short as had been the period since it had first been excited to mobility, it would gladly accept the sacrifice of its peerless maidenhead, and admit the stalwart prick of that happy lover who, alone of men born of women, will have the delicious privilege of carrying the light of knowledge to its hottest depths, I." "Oh, enough,

enough!" I cried laughingly, putting up my hand to stop her torrent of words, "I am delighted you told Gladys all this, and oh, Lucia, I do long! I do long for that perfect knowledge which you have so eloquently described."

"And your longing shall soon, very soon be indulged," cried Lucia. "Oh, we must hurry up old Penwick, and perhaps within a week my Susan shall have had not only one, but twenty, thirty, forty good, solid, succulent fucks!"

I bounded on, leaping and running, so great was my excitement. Never, never, was a girl more madly happy than I to hear this, and yet hardly twenty four hours had elapsed since, to all intents and purposes, my now raging cunt was dead asleep. Oh, how wide awake it was now!

I asked Lucia to let me read Gladys' letter once more. It interested me, but I did not understand the whole of it.

"What does she mean by our guests, Lucia?"

"Oh, they are people, ladies and gentlemen, but chiefly married ladies who, wishing for a change of diet, long for flesh pots they don't find in their husbands' beds – in other words, married ladies who fall in love with other men. They find it difficult to indulge their very natural passions in their own houses, still more difficult to do so in the houses of their lovers, and are afraid to go to hotels for fear of being recognised by other visitors there. We know so many people in high society that we know those whom we can trust, and there are ladies amongst our friends who sympathise with the anguish of lovers panting to enjoy a good fuck, and we permit our house to be named as a safe Bower of Bliss, where snug rooms, and comfortable beds, and perfect incognito can be found. We get a note, say a day or two before the happy night fixed upon for the full enjoyment. Gladys or I meet the lady, as it were by accident, at our friend's house, and the matter is quietly arranged. We ask the lady to dinner, she gets another invitation from our mutual friend to a quiet ladies' party at her house, she accepts the latter, tells her husband she is going there, but comes to us instead. Her beau, if we don't know him at first, comes to our house at dinner time, mentions the name which his lady is fixed on to bear in our house, and is admitted as a matter of course. We sometimes sit down to dinner as a party of eighteen or twenty; five of the twenty may be my lover, Gladys', Annette's, Gladys, and I; the remainder would be seven couples who come to enjoy a sweet half or whole night in one another's embraces, and the odd are either a guest, a lady friend, or a gentleman for whom we can't provide a bed and a cunt."

"And do these different couples know that the others are also going to fuck, Lucia?"

"Not unless they have intimate acquaintance with one another. Our rule is that when at the table, or in the drawing room, only the manners of society as it exists are to rule – i.e, there must be no amorous talk or play. A stranger would have no idea that anything more than a social meeting was intended, and I can assure you our reunions are delightful, as everyone is in a state of excitement more or less subdued, and all are expecting a delicious time in a few short hours. You will see that about 10 o'clock, as the time goes, people will rise to go away. Gladys will press them to give her the pleasure of their company for a little longer. They will excuse themselves, but as they leave the room, they go upstairs instead of down; and after the ladies have had a few minutes' grace, to arrange such little matters as they would not care to settle in the presence of their lovers, the gentlemen follow, discreetly kept from treading on one another's heels by either myself, Gladys, or Annette, who keep them in conversation until the coast is clear, when a gentle 'goodnight' and pressure of the hand tells them they can safely go to the rooms where their respective ladies are undressing and preparing to receive them."

"So in that way, I suppose, you prevent one gentleman seeing where another goes?"

"Quite so; not only that, but we are so clever that no gentleman sees another go upstairs at all."

"And how do they know their rooms, because if they are strangers to the house, and there are so many bedrooms, how can they avoid making a mistake?"

"That is very simple. We tell their ladies to give them the hint at dinner. In each guest's wine glass is put a flower, different to any other in the room: say one is a carnation, another a rose, another a lily or whatever you like. When the gentleman goes upstairs, he looks for a door having his flower in the keyhole, and opens it, walks in, and there is his lady, more or less undressed. Nothing can be more simple or well contrived, my dear Susan."

"But surely they must notice that every keyhole has a flower in it! And would not that make them suspect that others were on the same errand as themselves?"

"Oh, my darling Susan, you may be sure that men and women of the world have an immense amount of discretion, and don't see more than is needful. No doubt they do see a lot, but they say nothing, and, as a matter of fact, everybody minds his own affairs. We never have any trouble. Our guests must be well recommended, or else they would get no invitations, and the recommendations we get come from the highest quarters!"

"But," I persisted, as idea after idea presented itself to my mind, "it must put you to a lot of expense, all these dinners and entertainments."

"So it does," replied Lucia, with gentle acquiescence, "but Gladys is rich, and so am I, and even if we wished it we cannot prevent very handsome presents being made us, not only by our own lovers, but by those who reap the advantage of acquaintance with us: all goes to help, but our motives are not mercenary – we live the merriest, most delightful of lives, and what we do is from a love of pleasure. You see, we have no object on which to spend the seven or eight thousand a year we have between us, and so we can afford to be generous to Love. As it is, we do not spend half our income."

"Ah, that explains it all," I said, "but tell me, Lucia, who is Annette, whom you mentioned just now?"

"She is our confidential maid, a most lovely girl, whom a young Henry Pendleton seduced; she was his sister's maid. I took his maidenhead, and he continued by taking Annette's, but unfortunately his mamma found her in his bed, and turned her out of doors then and there. Her parents, being strict Presbyterians, would not take her back, and she would have gone on the streets as a last resort, or drowned herself, had not poor Henry, in a state of anguish, for he is a dear, kind hearted boy, written and implored me to help Annette. I sent for her and saw her. Her exceeding beauty at once recommended her to me, and I took her on as my own maid. Little by little I found she was as amorous as a pigeon and I proposed to her to admit a lover of mine, whom I could not take because another had a pre-engagement with me one night. She was delighted, and I heard such an excellent report of her next morning that I took her on as my *aide–de–con*!"

"*Aide–de–camp*!" said I, "Lucia, you don't pronounce it properly!"

"Don't I, dear? Well, I think I do! Con is the French for cunt, and I say truly when I say that Annette is my *aide–de–con*!"

I laughed, and was delighted at this new kind of staff appointment!

"So, I suppose, I am an *aide–de–con* that is to be, Lucia?"

"Of course, darling, if you like to look on it that way; but I hope you will always remember that, whereas by her agreement Annette must take any man we give her, you come to fuck, or not, as you please. You are, and will be, entirely your own mistress in that respect. We shall introduce gentlemen to you, and it is for you to introduce them or not, as you please, into your charming little cunt!"

"Oh, I don't think I shall raise many objections," said I, laughing.

"Nor does Annette! She is as lewd and lascivious as I am, and that is saying a good deal, my Susan!"

In this delightful manner we wandered on, chatting and laughing, and picturing all kinds of lovely events, when our conversation turned once more on the danger of unprotected fucking, a subject Lucia was extremely anxious to bring well home to my mind, and when once more she commenced holding forth about those most interesting but dangerous little atomies, tadpoles in the spend of a man, I said to her,

"Lucia, you talk as if you had actually seen the horrid little things!"

"So I have!"

"How?"

"Through a microscope, darling!"

"But how? When?"

"I will tell you," said she. "But here is a nice shady place. Sit down, and try not to grow so red as you did over the picture of Charlie Althair's prick!"

"Oh, do let me see those pictures again! I can listen whilst you tell me all about the tadpoles!" "Most appropriately, too, Susan, for it was from Charlie Althair's balls that they came!"

"Was it now, really?" I exclaimed, as I once more gazed with extraordinary pleasure on their vivid-looking portraits, "From these dear balls! Oh, how I shall like to see the real articles myself some day!"

"So you will, Susan darling, and soon! Do you know, I have been thinking that as Charlie Althair took my maidenhead, it would be as well if he had yours also, Susan! What do you think? Of course you have a perfect right to do with your own what you like, and maybe you might prefer some other man than Charlie to do that pleasant job for you. You have only to say frankly what you wish. It would be easy to have a half dozen handsome young bucks for you to make your choice from."

"Oh, Lucia!" I said, feeling half suffocated as the reality of the nearness of what I now most longed for became more and more apparent, "I don't think I can hesitate. It is true I don't know my cousin Charlie very well; still, I have seen him, and he has kissed me, when I was a little girl and he was growing up into a young man. I think we should look upon this as a family matter, and settle it in the family; so I think I'll give Charlie my maidenhead, if he thinks it worth the plucking!"

"If he thinks it worth the plucking!" exclaimed Lucia. "My dearest Susan, if we only had time, I should say, let Charlie beg and implore on his knees for such a priceless boon as the granting him a fuck at all! But it is imperative if you are to join us, that you should commence operations at once, and as before any real work can be done, your maidenhead must go, I say let Charlie have it. He is a dear, nice fellow, a splendid bedfellow, and I don't know any man I could better recommend to you, darling!"

"Very well, then that is settled, Lucia. But do tell me now about how you saw the tadpoles!"

"Well," she said, "about eighteen months ago, that is some time in the early spring of last year, Charlie came to see us in Park Lane, where we had gone to prepare for the London season. Frank Holt, the famous portrait painter, had just finished my picture, and we had invited him and a few of our most intimate and trusted friends to see it. Charlie had written to say he was afraid he could not come then, as he had an engagement in the country; in fact, as usual, he was after a virgin, and was fast bringing her to hear reason, and he could not afford to leave her just when he was apparently on the point of victory. Now, Charlie is one of the very best-hearted fellows going. There is a girl, a clergyman's daughter, Clara Dobbs, whom he had induced to take him between her thighs some twelve months previously, a fine, handsome creature, very spirited, amorous and passionately fond of fucking; a girl in fact, whom we all like, and who, when she heard of the advantages of our society, required no pressure to make her join it *con amore*. It was easy for people in our position to make the acquaintance of her father and mother down in Buckinghamshire, and they, good simple folk, were easily induced to let Clara visit her rich and fashionable London friends.

We have had her father and mother up, too, to stay with us with Clara, and that, too, at times when we might have seven or eight beds occupied by amorous couples, one of them having Clara herself in it with Charlie Althair or some other fine young fellow, and you may judge how extremely well everything went off, and how well we managed things, when our guests, the Dobbs, old people, never smelt a rat, and imagined the house was fast asleep, whilst the most lively performances, in which their own daughter was playing her part, were going on!"

"But, Lucia, what has this to do with the tadpoles, dear?"

"Now, Susan, have patience. You must always let me tell my story in my own way."

"I beg your pardon, darling! I won't interrupt again – it is really most interesting. You are very, very clever people."

"Well, as I said before, it was Charlie who first taught Clara how to fuck, and gave her that taste for it which will never fade as long as her cunnie retains its lively powers. He was exceedingly proud of having gained this maidenhead, because Clara had been really very strictly brought up, was old enough to know all about the relations of the sexes, and was in fact not at all a girl to be surprised by her senses into any false step. It took Charlie nearly three months of the most careful and assiduous attention to bring her to see the joy she might have if she admitted him to her bed, but at last she did, and it was in her own father's house that Charlie assailed her lovely cunt, and took the maidenhead she had guarded so well. From that day, or night rather, Clara never lost an opportunity of being fucked. Charlie took care of her, taught her all that was needful to know so as to keep herself safe, but as she, at first, had no man but him, she had no necessity to guard herself. Charlie did that for her. However, after she joined us, and became an associate, she fucked very freely with all the men we introduced to her. Amongst these is Allan MacAllan, a huge Highlander, a magnificent man, a great bull, a regular satisfying Hercules, exactly what we women like to find, a man big and powerful. But unfortunately Allan is selfish in so far as so long as he gets what he wants, he is not very particular in looking after the safety of the woman he has been having, in regard to the chances of her being exposed to have a baby. We therefore always cautioned Clara against him, but naturally, like all of us, she liked so fine a man as Allan, and would always choose him for her bedfellow, even before Charlie, if she had the chance. Now you know enough to understand what is going to follow.

"Well, to our surprise then, Charlie turned up early, that is, about lunchtime of the day we were giving our little rout in honour of my portrait being finished. We had arranged our party so that none but our most intimate and trusted friends should be there, all were to be associates, and there was to be a very delightful night spent in worshipping Venus. Consequently we had no girl for Charlie, unless we took Annette's man from her, and this we did not like to do. We told Charlie how sorry we were, and blew him up for not letting us know in time that he was coming, when we could so easily have had a nice, sweet little cunt for him, and then we asked him if he had been successful, and scored the maidenhead he was in chase of. He laughed and thanked us and said the maidenhead was still as intact as ever, as far as he knew, and that for the present he had to drop the pursuit, but that he hoped to take it up again very soon. Then he said, 'Oh, dear girls! I am sure you will be very much grieved to hear it, but Clara Dobbs is in the family way.'

"'Oh! No! Oh! no!' we screamed. 'How can that be? Are you certain, Charlie?'

"'I'm as sure as can be, I am as certain of it as I am that I have had both of you, Gladys and Lucia; as certain of it as that I took Clara's maidenhead.'

"We were most dreadfully shocked. This is how Charlie told us. He said, 'I was to have added another maidenhead to my list the night before last, everything was prepared, Julia Lawrence had consented at last and was eager to give it to me, when I got these letters. The first ran:

"'Dear Mr. Althair,
Papa and mamma desire me to ask you to come and dine and stay the night here, unless your engagements prevent you. You are to be scolded for coming to our part of the country without making our house your home. It was quite by accident that we learnt that you are staying at the Swan. Mamma begs me to say she hopes you will not disappoint us. With papa's and mamma's kind regards.
"'Believe me, yours truly,
"'Clara Dobbs."

"'Enclosed in this was another letter, which was couched in these words:

"'Dearest Charlie,
"'Believe me, I would not beseech and pray you to come and spend the night with me, knowing as I do how near you are getting the prize you have so long been striving after, only that it is a matter or life and death with me. I have most fearful news to tell you, and it can't be delayed. I entreat you, dearest Charlie, to remember that I gave myself to you before you ever knew Julia, and by the maidenhead which you reaped then I beseech you to come to your most unhappy, unfortunate Clara."

"'Well,' said Charlie, 'if Clara had not had heaps of fellows after me, I should have thought it was jealousy on her part; if she had not, herself, helped me to fuck other girls than herself, I should have refused to listen to her. A fellow can't very easily tell a maiden who has at last consented to have him, that he can't conveniently do it then, and I was at my wits' end to know what to say. Julia was to be at the Swan that evening with her people, who did not, and were not to know that I was there but everything was cut and dried, the head chambermaid was my ally, and everything would have gone well; I should have had a night of delight in Julia's arms but for this unhappy letter. I therefore returned at once, whilst there was time, to London, to send myself a telegram, saying my mother was extremely ill and supposed to be dying, and then returned to the Swan, got my telegram, put it in a despairing note for Julia which I gave to the chambermaid to give her on her arrival, and then I drove to the Rectory. I have not yet heard how Julia took the news, but I am certain she must have spent a most unhappy night.

"'The Dobbs' were awfully glad to see me, and easily accepted my excuses for not calling on them. Clara looked beautiful and radiant as ever, and I could see no sign of the frightful woe which, according to her letter, she ought to have been in, as it was a matter of life and death with her. I declare it took all my powers of self control to prevent my showing how desperately disinclined I was to stay in the house. The hour when Julia was to be at the hotel was dreadful to me when it came, and to think that she was within a quarter of a mile from me, and that all I had to do was to walk over, wait a little, and find myself, at 11 o'clock that night, between thighs which I burned to lie between, enjoying a sweet and lovely cunt which no man but I had as yet even felt with his hand, or fucked with his finger; her darling little maidenhead seemed to pull at the finger which had felt it, as much as to say "I am here! come and pluck me," and I heard the soft amorous voice again saying to me, "We shall be at the Swan on the 13th of this month. Come then and you shall have me if you don't change your mind between this and then." God! it was awful! Yet I bore it all! At last bedtime came. Clara pressed my hand and whispered "in an hour", and that hour, I, of course, had to wait, turning about on my bed until it would be quite safe to go to her. Dear girls, I suffered agony of mind and body, thinking of Julia in her bed, and no chance of going to her. I almost doubted Clara. I thought it might only be a trick, and I vowed if it was I would leave her and go off to the Swan, if I had to risk dropping twenty feet from my window to the ground to get out of the house. But when the time had come for saying goodnight, Clara had pressed my hand, and said in a low tone, "Come to my room in an hour when all is quiet. I have something dreadful to tell you," and the light and youthful expression which had been in her face all the evening up to this time departed, her eyes grew dark and mournful, and her mouth expressed a dangerous tendency to sobbing. I had returned her pressure with an "I will," and she went upstairs. Of course I knew that whatever it might be that Clara was about to tell me, I should be most of the night in her bed and that she would expect me to fuck her, so I undressed, and when all was quiet, I went to Clara's room. She was not in bed. She was undressed and in her night shift, and the moment I entered and had shut the door, she ran to me and clasped me in her arms, and pressing me to her bosom, burst into an agony of weeping, which alarmed me so much that my prick ceased to be stiff but hung at half cock.

"'What is the matter, Clara dear?' said I. 'Come, tell me!'

"'O! Charlie,' she said. 'It is too dreadful, and I know you will blame me. But indeed, I could not help it!'

"'But what is it, Clara?" She cried, she sobbed. She clasped me with desperate energy. Her lovely bubbies pressed my bosom and excited me. Up went my prick again, but the point of it seemed to me to strike her belly further in than it usually did on such occasions. I put down my hand to help it up, so as to get it between her belly and mine and give it a sweet squeeze between us when the cause of poor Clara's grief and despair instantly betrayed itself! That charming belly was, oh! much too rounded and full!

"'Oh! Clara!' I cried, 'Are you in pod?'

"'Yes, yes. Charlie. Oh, what am I to do? What am I to do?'

"'What brute put you in this state?' said I feeling her big belly, whilst, strange to say, my prick grew stiffer and stiffer, as though the idea of a baby being inside the girl made her cunt all the more desirable!

"'I am sure it was Allan MacAllan! I could not at first think who it was, I have had so many men, but I remembered that the last time Allan fucked me he had postponed using the sponge on the mantelpiece, and then we went to sleep. In the morning when we woke he had me again, but would neither get the sponge nor let me, and oh, Charlie, he is such a grand poke! I half believed him when he said that after such a lot of spend as he had given me overnight, he would not have much left. Alas, he had! His last spends (and he fucked me three times before we got up) were quite as plentiful as his first. Oh, fool that I was not to have got up at once after the first fuck, but it was so delicious to be in bed with him that I entirely forget prudence, and here is the result! I am certain it was Allan!'

"'But Clara!' said I. 'You may be mistaken You may not be really in the family way!'

"'Oh, I know I am Charlie! I am six months gone and I can feel the baby kicking inside me! Here, give me your hand. Do you feel that?' I did! Oh, there was no doubt at all! A fine, vigorous baby was at that moment plunging inside his unfortunate mother, and I could feel all his movements, which were dreadfully lively.

"'Poor Clara! I made her go to bed, and I got in with her. She let me see her belly, which was much bigger than I had ever seen before, and it looked as if its beautiful white skin was all stretched and polished from excessive fulness. Her breasts, too, looked changed. She made no objection to my fucking her. Indeed, she said she was only too glad to have me, as it might be the last time she would ever know rapture again. I almost forgot Julia! I don't think I ever enjoyed Clara so much before, and she said she had never felt so full of desire, or so sensitive to the pleasure my prick gave her as that night. During the intervals we formed all kinds of desperate plans but alas, always when we seemed at the point of finding one feasible, by which she might escape, an unthought-of obstacle always reared its poisonous head. All she gained from me was a night of really good fucking, but I left her as much in despair as ever. And now, girls, every day is precious!

"'There is no time to be lost. What is Clara to do?'

"We were nonplussed, Gladys and I.

"Never had such a dire misfortune occurred before. We could only chatter, we could not all at once hit on a plan. Gladys, who has more quiet good sense than I have, said she would invite a doctor friend of hers to come and sleep with her, and would consult him during the interval, and then our conversation fell upon the dangerous tadpoles which live in the balls of men. We had read of them, but we had never seen them, and were saying we would like to see what they were like, when Charlie's eye fell on a microscope on the drawing room table. 'Girls!' he cried, 'Nothing can be easier than to show you the tadpoles. That is, if that microscope is powerful enough.' He jumped up, and took the glass cover off it, put in a slide, looked at it and exclaimed that it would do.

"'Now!' said he, carefully lifting the instrument, 'Let us go into your foutoir, Lucia, and you shall make me spend, and I will show you the tadpoles.'

"Both Gladys and I were as excited as could be; we had had the microscope a long time, but the idea of utilising it in this way had never struck us before; we knew all about spermatozoa, theoretically, and we knew how to protect our wombs from the pestilent little objects, but we had never thought of trying to see with our eyes what they were like. I know I clapped my hands, and at the same time the idea of the whole thing made me feel more than randy. My cunt jumped and leaped, and Gladys called out at the redness of my cheeks.

Charlie led the way he knew my foutoir well. Oh! had he not fucked me there often enough? Frank Holt was to have me for the first time that night, there also, as a reward for painting my portrait. Oh, Susan, he must paint you too. You should see what a lovely picture he will make, and mind! He will give you your bush and cunt as large and as plain as life!

"When Charlie saw the picture of me hanging over the mantelpiece he laid down the microscope and exclaimed at the beauty of it. Frank has made me as a girl going for her morning bath in a clear stream. I am first looking round, as I throw off my robe, and I am in the act of coming down some steps which lead through tall reeds under the shade of a tree to the limpid water. The spectator's eye is supposed to be on a level with my knees, so that he can, by just looking up, see all those beauties which lie between my thighs. Charlie was in raptures. It was the best painted cunt he said he had ever seen, and turning to me he said, 'Lucia, let us compare the original with the portrait!'

"'All right,' said I, laughing, 'But I don't believe Frank Holt has idealised it at all,' and I at once commenced undressing.

"'Wait!' cried Gladys. 'It would be as well that Annette saw the tadpoles too. I will ring for her!'

"'Well,' said Charlie, 'now I tell you what! Let's us have a quartet. Gladys, you strip too! Annette will also; so will I, and we will have a sacrifice in honour of science, which the very gods will appreciate.'

I clapped my hands, for I saw what must be the inevitable result, and Gladys in her quiet way got three sponges ready. You may be sure Annette made no opposition, and very soon there we were, all four, as naked as we were born. Charlie said the picture was certainly lovely, but that it had not, to his idea, done me full justice, and that my real flesh and blood cunt was worth fifty of its portraits in oil or water colour. Then we arranged how to make Charlie spend, for, of course, it would not do for him to lose it in any of our cunts. At first Gladys proposed he should fuck each of us, taking care not to spend in any of us, but when he felt himself coming, to snatch himself out of the cunt he might be in at that moment, but Charlie himself said, 'No!' He said when once he got near the short digs he must continue, and he could not withdraw from a cunt which was giving him rapture even if its owner consented, a thing he greatly doubted. A little thought convinced us of the truth of his remarks. So this was how we managed.

'Gladys sat on the ottoman, which is very large and soft, and with her back supported, opened her thighs wide so that Charlie might lie back along her belly with his head on her bubbies and his arms round her thighs. He could thus feel her bush somewhere about the middle of his back.

Annette, kneeling between his legs, was to caress his balls, whilst he gazed at her lovely, white bosom and its rich and beautiful snowy globes, whilst I, kneeling on one side of him, was to manipulate his splendid prick, with my hand moving up and down, and have a cup ready to catch his spend when it came. I declare it was most voluptuous. Oh, Susan how you will like feeling a splendid prick! I worked Charlie's with all the voluptuous ardour I could command. He seemed to think it delicious. He soon gave up looking at anything.

He half shut his eyes, and his parted lips showed how great his pleasure was. Suddenly he called out 'Quick! Quicker! Lucia!' I hastened my movements, my hand flew up and down his prick and, with a burst, the torrent of creamy spend shot up like a fountain, falling in its first jet upon Gladys' bosom, in its second on to Charlie's, and then, each getting less and less strong, it finally poured all hot and scalding over my hand! And I had quite forgotten to try and catch any in the cup!

"For a few seconds we all remained as still as statues. I was amazed at the quantity of spend which had come from Charlie and also the tremendous force with which he had ejaculated it, and I fancy Gladys and Annette were quite as much surprised as I was; for was it not funny, darling, when you come to think of it?

Neither of us, not one of us three girls had ever seen a man spend before, though we had often seen the spend itself and felt it dashing into us hundreds and hundreds of times! I have to tell you something still more funny directly. Well, after a little while, Charlie, who had been lying still with his eyes shut and with the most placid expression of complete enjoyment on his face suddenly looked up and said, 'Thank you, Lucia dear. Your little hand is almost as nice and as soft as your sweet little cunt! But I like your cunt best.'

"Then he looked into the cup, which I still held up in my left hand, for my right was still grasping his grand prick, which was jerking from time to time powerfully, just as I had felt it often when it was in me after a good poke.

"'Why,' he exclaimed, 'you have not got a drop in the cup, Lucia! Where did it all go?'

"'Some on me,' said Gladys in her quiet voice, 'but most on yourself, Charlie dear.'

"Charlie then looked down, and seeing his body all wet, especially his belly and bush, said it did not much matter if none went into the cup, because one drop would be quite sufficient.

"'One drop!' I cried.

"'Yes, one drop!' said Charlie, getting up. 'Oh,' he said, 'Look here! Look at Gladys' bush! There is a regular little pool just resting on it, which has not soaked in amongst the hairs yet!'

"And so there was. The first shower Gladys got had been stopped from flowing down her body by Charlie's shoulders, but when he got up it had been trickling down between her bubbies and along her belly, and was like a little pool of cream looking bluish white against her coal-black bush!

"Charlie got a slide with a little hollow in it, and a little tube of glass, and picking up a drop of his spend off Gladys, put it on the slide, and then moved to the microscope, through which he looked. After a second or so he called out, 'Come girls! Come and see the varmints!'

"Oh, Susan! I had first look. The drop under the microscope was not so big as an ordinary tear, and yet it was alive with spermatozoa. There they were, hundreds of them, like little grey tadpoles, head and tail exactly the same, and wriggling about in a way which made me shudder.

"'Now!' said Charlie to me, 'One of those, if it got into the right place, Lucia, would do your business, and you would have a child!'"

I, Susan Aked, shuddered when I heard it!

"Oh, Lucia, what terrible dangers you must have run."

"Well, yes and no. Listen. After we had all seen the living tadpoles, Charlie proposed to show us those which had been exposed to the liquid in the sponges, and to do that said he had better fuck one of us.

"Gladys said 'We are all ready, Charlie! You must go the rounds, my dear boy.'

"'Yes, yes!' I cried. 'Have us one after another, Charlie, and what do you say, Gladys? Won't it be a good plan if, to make all things equal, Charlie withdraws the moment he makes one of us spend, and then goes to the next, makes her spend, and then the next, makes her spend, and then to the first, and so on until he spends himself?'

"Annette clapped her hands, and ran to the ottoman and lay back on it with her lovely thighs – such splendid thighs, Susan – open and ready for Charlie the moment he came.

"Oh, that was such fun. Charlie began with Gladys. Gladys had him for a very few strokes, because she spends very quickly. Then he went to Annette, who comes nearly as quickly as Gladys. And last to me; and I got the rapturous short digs! After our thorough enjoyment of what I may call the afterglow of a luscious fuck, Charlie withdrew his prick, and then, getting a slide, he gently pulled out my sponge by the thread, when, of course, all the spend in me flowed over it, his and mine mixed together. 'Now,' said he, 'come and look at this!'

As I had been the one most interested I was allowed first peep. There they were indeed, the nasty, dangerous little tadpoles, but barely a sign of life in one of them. They were all dead as door nails!"

"Really and truly?"

"Really and truly! Oh! I can tell you, Susan, we three girls were glad to see it. I do believe we should have been frightened after poor Clara's accident, but for what Charlie showed us. And after each of the other two pokes he gave us, it was just the same, though the liquid in my sponge had not been renewed, for I had the great good luck to be the one in whom Charlie spent each time."

"And you were not frightened?"

"Oh, not a bit after what I had seen. But oh, Susan, I told you I had never seen a man spend before that day. Well, fancy. I had never seen a man fuck a woman before! It is such a fetching sight! The most fetching part is when he is getting the last half inch or so in. The way his hips sink between her thighs, as he presses his motte to hers, is, oh, beyond anything voluptuous in the extreme! Ah, how I did enjoy that afternoon, and indeed I had good fun with Frank Holt afterwards!"

"Was he a good poke, Lucia?"

"Upon my word he was, Susan! He is considerably over fifty, and I never expected more than two grinds from him, and neither of them really good! Whereas he gave me six good, solid, real good fucks before he slept, and one more in the morning, and he knows how to do it, too! He must have been superb when he was young,"

"Tell me, Lucia darling, what did you do about poor Clara?"

"Oh, Gladys slept with her doctor, and after an awful lot of trouble got him to promise to perform an operation on Clara, in our house. We invited her up, and Gladys put her under chloroform, so that she might not see who worked upon her poor little quim, and the doctor did it as cleverly as could be. The child was born dead, and Clara was relieved; but she was as near dying as could be. Such bleeding set in, it took all the doctor knew to stop it, but she was saved, and luckily her parents believed her story about her spraining her ankle, and never came to town to see after her, believing her to be in such good hands when she was with us! She soon got well, and would you believe it, the very first man she had on her recovery was Allan Mac Allan!"

"Oh!"

"Yes! But we gave him such a lecturing that I don't think he'll ever ' pooh pooh' the saviour sponge again."

CHAPTER V
FRUITION

Lucia's story of the tadpoles affected me in more ways than one. I shivered alternately with fright and pleasure. I was something like a person suffering from ague – I had my cold fit succeeded by the hot. At one time I thought that not for all the pleasure in the world would I run the risk of giving admittance to no matter how charming a prick, which would surely leave behind it myriads of these disgusting tadpoles, each one of which constituted a danger of the very greatest importance to me.

On the other hand, the fact that Lucia had not hesitated to give herself to Charlie the very minute after he had shown her the nasty, wriggling things through the microscope, showed that however great the danger from them might be, she felt convinced that she was so well protected that they could do her no harm, even though she were inundated by an ocean swarming with them. We talked and talked about them until my confidence began to return and I was once more in that state of enraptured expectation that, had Charlie come in, I should not have hesitated to take him between my thighs!

Dear reader! I do so regret that I must bring my story to a close just when, in fact, it is only commencing, but I am the victim of circumstances, at the moment necessitating a long journey, and I do not know but that I may be called upon to travel, at all events to shift from place to place, for so long a time that I may not easily find leisure to continue these memoirs, so delightful for me to write and, I trust, pleasant and instructive to read.

Our visit to Worcester took place, and afforded Lucia an opportunity of dilating upon the handsome cousin who was to be my first lover! We drove past the place where the Althairs used to live, and Lucia pointed out to me where she and Charlie had many a sweet *al fresco* encounter. Oh dear, what a lad Charlie must have been! It was in that house he commenced his career as a lover of women! In that house he committed his first rape! In that house he laid the foundation of his first baby, for the ladies have at times used my cousin Charlie as a stallion when it was their wish to have offspring. And all about Worcester there were sites, sacred to the delicious consummation of love and desire, in which Charlie had been the man, and oh, a great variety of maids and matrons the women! Lucia seemed to have been the repository of all my cousin Charlie's amatory secrets, and her retailing them to me, with all the names of the fair ladies who had surrendered their charms to him told me more forcibly than anything could how great was the confidence she reposed in me.

I had intended to have made my dear readers acquainted with, at all events, the outlines of these exciting stories, but, alas, I have not the time. I must hurry on, and describe how I put in practice all that Lucia had taught me, and how I surrendered my maidenhead, and learnt the rapture which man, and man alone, can give to woman.

We paid our intended visit to old Penwick, and persuaded him to let me go to London sooner than he had at first thought possible, on the promise that, if I should be required at Worcester I could return without fail or delay. Lucia also ordered some dresses for me. She got me what she called "decent" drawers, chemises and stays, and in a very few days we were ready and started for London.

It was early in August. Few people were travelling to London, that is in the first-class compartments, so that we had the carriage almost entirely to ourselves the whole way.

Lucia, expectant of the delight she most prized on earth, was bursting with joy, and radiant with pleasure. We were to have only a "family" party. Allan MacAllan was to be Lucia's man; Sir James Winslow, Gladys"; Robert Dane, Annette's; and Charlie Althair mine. Not for one moment did Lucia leave me to my thoughts; she either by design, or because she really was so excited herself, kept chatting, chatting, chatting to me, and always on the subject of the pleasure, so that, what with her words and the vivid caresses she continually gave me, I was in a state bordering almost on mania when we at length reached London. Had Charlie met us on the platform he might have taken me into the ladies" waiting room and had me there and then, and I should have offered not the slightest resistance. Lucia had continued to make me so lewdly randy – there is no other word to express my sensations. My heart and my cunt were on fire, and my blood ran like a torrent of fire through my throbbing veins.

A very handsome carriage and pair driven by a coachman in a splendid livery, and with a footman also, met us at Euston. Lucia spoke kindly and gently to both of the men, who touched their hats, and seemed glad to see her again. I looked keenly at them to see whether anything in their deportment showed that want of respect which, I had been taught to believe, marked the knowledge by men of their mistresses not being all they should be. But I saw nothing but the most well-bred respect, married with that affection which all good and well-trained servants show towards employers whom they love. In the state I was in, I could almost have given myself then and there to the footman, for he was a really handsome, well–made young man, and quite fit, as far as personal qualifications were concerned, to lie between a lady's thighs. I don't see why a lady may not desire a handsome servant man, just as gentlemen most certainly desire handsome servant women, so that I do not feel at all ashamed of telling my dear readers of what my feelings were on this occasion.

We drove rapidly through street after street. In spite of my throbbing cunt and my beating heart, I could not but observe all that I saw, and the huge London, of which I was then seeing but a small portion, struck me with amazement. But the noise prevented much conversation and Lucia made me recline backwards, whilst the only way I knew how intense her feelings were, was from the repeated hard squeezes she gave my hand.

At length we reached Park Lane, and drew up in front of what, from the outside, seemed so modest looking a house that I was rather disappointed. I had expected to see a more palatial looking building after all Lucia's descriptions, but I forgot that she had described no more than the inside of the house to me.

A fine, well-preserved, elderly woman opened the door for us, and once we were inside, Lucia kissed her affectionately, and introduced me to her. The old lady shook my hand and said I was a fine, pretty creature.

"Who's at home, Sarah?" asked Lucia.

"Miss, Gladys is upstairs, Miss, and Mr Charlie Althair."

My face, I know, became crimson on hearing that name. Then he, he who was to–to–oh my goodness! He was already here!

Yes, indeed. At that moment I saw a lady coming down the stairs followed by a gentleman. The lady I guessed to be Gladys, and the gentleman I recognised to be my cousin Charlie, though it was years since I had last seen him, and he was only a boy then and I a little girl. But what a difference there was in him to what I recollected! There was a tall, broad-shouldered, strong-looking man, young indeed in face, but a perfect man in form and figure, instead of the slip of a handsome boy as I remembered my cousin Charlie. Now he had a fine moustache, and the firm-looking jaws of a man. I think the thing that perhaps struck me most was the appearance of power in him. He looked as if he could pick me up, and put me on his shoulder, and jump with ease over a five-barred gate. I felt my heart jump with admiration, and I was glad that such a splendid man as he was going to have me. I did not feel a bit shy. Lucia had wound me up to such a pitch that I was shivering with desire, and all the day since we commenced our journey I had had the most extraordinary sensation in the lower part of my body, in the "organs of Love", as though millions and millions of ants were creeping and crawling in and out of my cunt, and all over my motte and groin, whilst my breasts seemed to be swollen and itching to be handled and pressed.

Gladys, for it was she, glided you could not say walked, for her movement was more like that of a stately vessel wafted by a light breeze over smooth water to Lucia, and the two women embraced one another with hearty hugs and kisses, pressing their breasts together, first on one side, and then on the other. They only said a few words to one another. It was, "Well, Gladys!"

"Well, Lucia!"

Then they separated, and Lucia flew open-armed to Charlie, and oh, how they kissed and caressed one another! I felt a great pang of jealousy as I saw Lucia's hand fly to the top of Charlie's thighs, move about rapidly as if trying to find something, and at last get it, not at all where I expected she would have found it, but halfway up to his waistcoat! I felt as jealous as could be of the hot kisses I saw Charlie giving her, and of the joy I knew she must experience feeling his hand stroking her, as it did, between her thighs.

But Gladys, who perhaps noticed the shade on my face, came to me smiling, and gave me oh such a sweet kiss. What a mouth she had; what lips! It was a kiss which, woman as Gladys was, provoked desire even in me, who was, like her, all but a woman, for before midnight I expected I should be like her no longer a virgin!

I returned her embrace with fire. My kiss seemed to electrify Gladys, whose thighs locked with mine, and whose hand sought for and pressed my bubbies. She flushed as she said, "Ah, Susan, I see you are just what Lucia said you were! We shall be great friends, darling, I am sure. And how nicely you are made. You have quite a fine bosom, and I dare say," she added with a meaning smile, "you are as well made here." (she let her hand fall as low as possible and press against my motte. And I hope you have brought us an ornament which will be as much admired for its beauty and delightfulness as I am certain your face and figure will be!"

And she kissed me again and again, looked into my eyes with hers, and oh, what eyes she had! They seemed to warm into my very marrow, and to dart torrents of desire and all-voluptuous longings!

Our embraces, caresses and kisses, made me for the moment half forget Charlie and Lucia, for I am a creature of impulse, and if my senses are powerfully affected, as they were at the moment by the sensation of Gladys' electrifying and really delicious charms, I cannot help yielding up to them. What a blessing this is for me! Dear reader, all men are the same to me! Yet that one who holds me in his arms is, for the while, the perfection of mankind! I forget all the others whilst I enjoy his vigour, his manhood, and the rapturous pleasure his exquisite prick gives me.

But if I forgot, or half forgot, Charlie, Lucia did not forget me.

"There!" she said. "That's kissing and stroking enough, you two naughty girls! Gladys! Here is Charlie burning to know how his lovely cousin is made, and I am sure Susan would like to make his acquaintance, and that of holy Saint John Thomas, too!"

Gladys laughed, and I felt myself growing red-hot – not with shame, but with the immense pleasure I knew was before me. As I quitted the arms of the voluptuous girl, who had been adding fuel to the fire that devoured me, Charlie took me into his.

"How you have grown, Susan!" he said, as he kissed me, keeping his hot lips on my mouth, and passing his still hotter tongue along my lips from corner to corner.

"And so have you, Charlie dear," I answered, as soon as I had the use of my lips to speak.

Charlie held me at arm's length, whilst he looked at me with eager eyes. His two hands held me under the armpits, and whilst he gazed at me as though he had that one chance of doing so and never would again see me and wished to remember me, he gently and gradually brought his hands towards one another in front, and then pressed them on my swelling breasts.

"What good bubbies!" he cried, and then he suddenly turned me round, so that I had my back to him, and pulling my head back against his shoulder, he again snatched the most voluptuous kisses from my mouth and felt first one and then the other of my breasts. Goodness, how different did his strong hand feel to Lucia's or that of Gladys! Surely, some strange influence – perhaps the male influence – passed from his palm into my bubbies, and thence down to my burning cunnie!

I know it was quite different to being handled by Lucia, though, oh, what pleasure she used to give me when she squeezed my bosom with her soft hands!

"Come!" cried Lucia, who had been with Gladys watching all this with eyes dancing with excitement. "Come into the study, Charlie! Come, Susan, I want Charlie to assure himself, before me, that I deliver you a perfect maiden into his hands, and that you carry the warranty of your virginity in the pretty cushion between your thighs!"

Charlie put his arm round my waist and urged me towards the door through which Gladys and Lucia had passed, with eager but not unbecoming haste.

There was a large ottoman in this room (there were similar ottomans in every room in the house) and on this Lucia made us sit whilst she and Gladys stood before us.

"Now, first of all, Charlie, you must let me show Susan the Holy Saint who is to say his prayers in the niche prepared for him called her quim!

Charlie laughed and said, "Certainly."

Lucia with rapid fingers undid his waistcoat and his braces before and behind; then she unbuttoned his trousers down to the very last button, and, pulling up his shirt, produced what, to my heated imagination, seemed something much larger than I had ever expected to find a man's prick to be. Ah, how different is reality to imagination! I had had Charlie's beautiful prick before me in a picture, I had heard it described, I had formed an idea of its magnitude, bulk, length and power; but ardent as my imagination had been, minute Lucia's descriptions had been, the reality was vastly more splendid!

"There!" cried Lucia, as she put my hand onto the delicious, hot, hard, yet velvety-feeling weapon, round which my eager fingers could hardly meet. "That is the prick which took my maidenhead, Susan, and which will take yours! Oh, beautiful Saint John! Oh, glorious Saint John! Is it not grand, Susan? Now, is it not as delicious to feel as I told you it would be? But wait until you feel it walking up and down your little silky cunt, my dear. Oh, goodness! How I wish I had my first fuck to do again! Now, here! Put your hand in and get out the bag of jewels."

I did so. I looked at Charlie, who bent his head forward, and as our mouths met, I had his magnificent balls in my hand. Oh, how nice, how extra voluptuous they did feel. There is something in the balls of a man which is more fascinating, more captivating than even his glorious prick in all its glory. Is it because his balls are the evidence of his manhood? I can't tell but I only know that I never tire of feeling a good pair; and I had, at that moment, a splendid, full, hard, big pair of them in my fingers, and could feel them slide from side to side, as I gently pressed them.

"Now, Charlie! Assure yourself of the existence of Susan's maidenhead," and Lucia lifted my dress, petticoats and all, high over my knees.

Charlie needed no hand to guide his to my throbbing cunt. He only held me a little more firmly while he just pressed his curved hand and finger over my bushy motte and the soft lips of my palpitating quim, and then, putting his tongue deep into my mouth, he slipped his strong middle finger as far as he could between the full, soft lips of a cunt which, except for Lucia's fingers and twat, had been virgin since it had been created.

Girls, dears! Wait until a lover does the same to you, and then you shall tell me if such caresses are, or are not exquisite!

"Well?" said Lucia, all avidity for Charlie's verdict.

"A perfect virgin," he exclaimed. A first-class maidenhead. There can be no doubt about that."

"And now has she not a delicious little cunt, Charlie?"

"Awfully good! Awfully nice!" was the answer, as his finger gently and sweetly worked up and down, killing me with pleasure.

"Let me feel her maidenhead!" said Gladys, coming forward.

Charlie instantly withdrew his hand and I saw Gladys give him what looked like a little packet of cigarettes. Then kissing me, she slipped her slender, long finger in, and smiling and flushing at the same time, said, "Oh, yea! Most distinct! A real and true maidenhead! And what a darling little quim. Charlie, I wish you every joy."

"Now, Gladys, I was the original discoverer of this wonderful virginity. So let me have a last feel of it, for I think it won't see the light of another day!" This was Lucia, of course, and her hand, oh, that dear little hand which had first made me aware of what immense resources of pleasure were concealed, unknown to me, in that dormant little cunt of mine, took the place of Gladys'.

But all these varying caresses, these different hands, these changing fingers, added to the state of intense excitement in all that highly susceptible region, produced a very natural, but apparently not expected, result. I had Charlie's glorious prick in my grasp again. It alone was capable, even so, of upsetting the equilibrium of my senses, but these fingers moving in and out...

"Oh, you naughty girl, Susan!" exclaimed Lucia. "Just look, Gladys, she has spent all over my hand."

"I am very sorry, Lucia. Indeed I could not help it," cried I, almost in distress.

"Never mind, darling," they all cried together, and Charlie again taking possession of my quivering cunnie, kissed me very passionately. I heard the door shut, and when Charlie gave one a chance of seeing, I found that we were alone. Gladys and Lucia had left the room.

"Susan!" whispered Charlie, in a voice husky with excitement; dear boy, he was always excited, tremendously excited, when on the brink of a nice plump cunt.

"Will you give me your maidenhead now? Ah, say yes! I could not wait till bedtime."

I raised my face and kissed him, and whispered, "Yes." With a bound Charlie jumped up. He left me lying across the ottoman. I heard a quick rustling of clothes, and there he was, with only his shirt and boots and socks on. Whilst I looked at him he tucked his shirt up so that all his body from his waist downwards to the top of his socks was absolutely and perfectly naked. Oh, how I longed to see him as Lucia had drawn him, with nothing on but his skin; what a handsome object a well made naked man is! How different in every way was he from the slender softness of Lucia. Charlie's muscles seemed like engines of great force, as every movement of his made them play under his white and even skin, and how white his skin did look. I had no idea a man's skin could be so white, and it looked all the whiter from the contrast of the dark black hairs which grew in parts wonderfully thick over his body, down the outsides of his thighs and down his legs.

But what naturally attracted my most eager attention was that magnificent, glorious, handsome prick of his. To my astonished vision it appeared to have grown even longer, bigger and more rigid than ever. It seemed to me, lying down as I was, to reach quite an inch up over his navel, and it was pointing straight up, apparently at his chin. I noticed then the curious shape of the underside of its well–shaped head, as if it had been carved by nature into two curves meeting near the top, and gracefully sweeping down and asunder, one curve taking the right and the other the left. The shape of that head appeared to make the noble weapon it tipped perfectly irresistible, and I could see how admirably nature had formed it for penetrating. But, oh, could I possibly take in that huge (for it did look so huge) thing?

Surely my cunt was neither deep enough, nor wide enough, to admit it all, and, as Lucia had told me, I noticed that it grew broader and broader as it approached its base. I saw too, all along the front, as it appeared to me, a kind of supporting rod under its tight-looking skin, and of this Lucia had not told me anything that I could remember. And below, hanging in that curiously wrinkled pouch, which looked as if it had been sewn up all along the middle, were those delicious balls which I had been feeling. How big they looked, and how evenly they seemed to hang, each in its own pocket as it were. And oh, what a splendid bush there was, out of which all these splendours grew. Far thicker and longer and much more curly than either Lucia's or mine.

Charlie saw admiration in my burning and excited glances, and he gave me time to note all. Then when he thought I had seen enough for the present he said, "Now, Susan, let me clear your decks for action!"

Oh, the swiftness of his hands! He had my dress and petticoats over my face in a trice. He tugged at the band of my drawers, and without mercy burst it. I heard the ripping and felt the tearing, as his powerful fingers tore through the linen, and the fresh feeling of the air on my belly and thighs told me that he had stripped the lower part of my body as naked as his own! I could not see, for my face was covered.

"Susan, darling!" he cried, his voice trembling. "Here, look! Take this and put it on me."

He handed me a curious-looking little thing which felt soft and elastic, and had a long deep line in it, for all the world like a little cunt. It was not thicker than an ordinary slate pencil, and about two inches long. I looked wonderingly at Charlie, for I did not, know what I was to do.

"There!" said he. "Take hold of me low down near my balls with your left hand. That's right. Now lay the letter on the top of my prick, only turn the other side (the cunt–shaped side) up. Now sweep your hand down, and that thing will open and cover me completely!"

I did exactly what he told me, and lo! There was his prick completely covered almost to its very end with a thin, transparent covering of india rubber, which looked like another natural skin! This, then, was the covering of which Lucia had told me. I declare if it had not been for seeing this I should never have thought of the dangerous tadpoles! I was so eager, so anxious to be fucked that I had altogether forgotten the very serious lessons which dear Lucia had given me.

"Thank you, dear Charlie!" I cried. "I know what this is for!"

"Lucia told you, I suppose?"

"Yes! She taught me everything!"

"You could not have a better instructor," said Charlie, "but now, my Susan, for experience!"

"Come!" cried I, lying back and opening my thighs wide, planting my feet firmly on the yielding ottoman.

In another moment, Charlie was between them and on me. I felt a thrill, not to be described for pleasure, as the soft-feeling yet powerful head, separating the lips of my throbbing little cunt, entered! The ease with which it penetrated astonished me. But it was in! In! I could feel it expanding and filling me as far as it had gone. But something inside me checked it, and Charlie, instead of trying to push it in any further, kept pushing his prick in and out, tickling me in so ravishing a manner that I held my breath to enjoy it the more. All my soul seemed concentrated at that one spot. Little throbs began to shoot all about it, and I knew I was on the point of coming! I expected every moment Charlie would plump deeper in; but he still continued his play, which was on the point of becoming disappointing, when I suddenly came!

Charlie had apparently waited for this, for the moment he perceived it he grasped me to him tighter than ever.

I felt a violent struggle going on. It was the expiring effort of my poor little maidenhead! Then something rent inside me, an extraordinary sensation of neither pain nor pleasure followed, the obstacle was overcome, and with alternate movements backwards and forwards I felt Charlie's prick rapidly gaining ground, and for the first time knew the infinite joy of being filled and stretched to the utmost by the power of man!

"Ah! Ah! Ah!" cried Charlie at each stroke, and his breath poured hot down my neck inside my collar. His balls touched me! I felt them! I bucked, and he was all in!

"You darling!" he cried, and then began the splendid, long strokes.

Gods! How nice it was! At first it did not tickle very much. The chief pleasure was feeling the alternating filling and contracting of my cunt, but after a few strokes the tickling from end to end began to grow more and more brilliant, until it seemed to me that I should faint from the excessive pleasure I experienced! There were perfect spasms, like electric shocks in their force and rapidity, which cannot be described; which, my dear girls, can only be experienced, and with all the most deliciously soothing sensations, feel indescribably delicious. Oh, my God! Was it not Rapture! Rapture with a very big 'R'!

But alas, the longest fuck is always too short and Charlie's time was come! All of a sudden he commenced those rapid, short digs which sent me wild with an agony of delight! My entire body glowed with the white heat of the glory of heaven! My senses reeled; all the room seemed to whirl round and round. I felt that in another moment I must faint, when, crushing me to him, Charlie for the last time dashed his prick into me to its very furthest limit, and I felt his whole weight on my pimping motte. I felt as if a powerful pump were sending streams in jets against me inside. One, two, three, four, I counted – there were more but I went into a half-swoon of ecstasy, and seemed to be quite lifted out of all connecting me with earth! I was in a kind of dream in which I saw angels floating around me, and felt the ineffable blessing of the peace of heaven.

But Lucia's laughing voice recalled me to earth, and I found myself still in Charlie's arms, and could feel his glorious prick in me, working, as if it were trying to burst my quivering cunnie by swelling itself out with repeated efforts.

"Well, Susan? Take your head out of the way, Charlie, and let me kiss my girl," and I heard a smart slap on my lover's bottom, which vibrated all along his prick and made my cunnie quiver. "There, there, my own darling Susan!" as she kissed me with impetuous kisses, "Not much of a maidenhead left now, I fancy. Did he hurt you, darling?"

"Hurt?" I exclaimed. "Hurt! Oh, how could it hurt me, Lucia dear?"

"Oh, all right," she exclaimed, laughing, "I am glad it did not, but sometimes it does."

"By George, Lucia," said Charlie, "I can tell you it is well Susan has no teeth in her quim, or deuce a bit of a prick would I have left. Oh, if you could only feel her now!"

"Has she the nutcrackers, then?" exclaimed a voice which I knew to be that of Gladys.

"Has she? If you were like me and in her, Gladys, you would soon know."

"Oh, Susan, Susan, you are an acquisition!" cried Gladys, moving from behind Charlie, where she had apparently been watching my behaviour, perhaps from the very beginning, for, once Charlie had begun to fuck me I had no senses to see or hear, and I don't know at what precise moment she and Lucia had returned to the room. She kissed me and petted me, and after a while, addressing Charlie, said: "Is she still nipping you, Charlie?"

"I think that was the last," said he.

"Very well. Get off her, then."

"Ah, but Susan has such an awfully nice quim. Let me enjoy it a little longer."

"Nonsense, boy. Get up, I tell you. It is time we all bathed and dressed for dinner."

"Ah well, I suppose I must. But oh, Susan, won't we just have a night of it? Do you like me, dear?"

Oh! I gave him such a kiss, and such a hug and such a sweet little buck, before he began to move, that he swore he never had had such a sweet, darling, responsive girl before in all his life.

"Did I not tell you she was a perfect diamond?" cried Lucia, delighted. Charlie slowly withdrew his ardent prick which, as it issued, sprang up as if it had been suddenly released from something holding it down, but the moment Gladys saw it she cried out, "Why, oh, my goodness, Charlie! Your letter has burst!"

And so it had. Charlie's prick was entirely through it. It was all rucked up about the middle of its shaft.

"Jump up, Susan; come with me," cried Gladys; and Lucia, taking me by the arm, pulled me in a way which rather alarmed me.

"Don't be frightened, darling," said Lucia, "but the sooner we get Charlie's spend out of you the better!"

I felt a great deal of it running out of me then. I could feel it running down my thighs, but the recollection of the tadpoles frightened me a bit, and I ran upstairs following Gladys as quickly as I could. She and Lucia took me into a handsome little boudoir, and through it into a fine bathroom where they made me tuck up my dress and petticoats, and sit on a small stool covered with American cloth, which felt very cool as I sat down on it. Lucia got a basin and put it between my feet, Gladys brought an enema and a bottle. Lucia got a small vessel and water, and in a wonderfully short time I had the tube in me, and a torrent of 'safety' liquid was cleaning from me that spend which had been so exquisitely pleasant to feel dashing into me.

Having tenderly wiped me between my thighs the two girls took me back into the boudoir, or as Lucia called it, the foutoir.

It was Gladys', and oh, so beautiful. That it was intended for the offices of love was instantly apparent. The wall was hung with beautiful pictures, some in oils, some in watercolours, some engravings and some beautifully executed pencil or crayon drawings, but all, whether large or small, were of the most exciting erotic nature. Venus and Adonis, Diana and Endymion, Jupiter and Leda, Jupiter and Danae and many other mythological love scenes were there, with innumerable others representing amorous couples under almost every conceivable circumstance. Even love in a carriage in Rotten Row was depicted, showing the possibility of a rapturous fuck in the very midst of a crowd. And all were really beautifully painted or drawn, by no means the work of an indifferent artist. A choice collection of erotic literature, some hundred volumes or so of prose and poetry, was in full view in a handsome bookcase. The very letter-weights on the writing-table were erotic – either human couples in the very act, or animals, such as a stallion and mare, bull and cow, and so forth. Of course there was an ottoman. How often, I wonder, has Gladys given some active lover of hers joy on it?

There we sat and talked for a while until the handsome Annette came and announced that the bath was ready.

Oh, my dear male readers! If you only could have seen the three lovely, naked nymphs who bathed their charms in that splendid marble basin; if you could but have seen the equally lovely handmaid in all her beautiful nudity, plying soap and sponge and towel – I include myself, for I know I am well made and pretty – I wonder which one of us would have made your blood boil the hottest and quickest. All four of us were dark-haired, and nature had been kind in giving us plenty of glory on our heads and on our mottes too.

Gladys' bush was the blackest. Her hair was really black. She was most splendidly formed. Such shoulders, such arms, such beautiful breasts and thighs. No wonder men delighted in her. She looked voluptuous from head to foot, and was as voluptuous as she looked.

Lucia had taught me what pleasure one girl can give another, but her caresses, ardent as they were, paled before the glory of those which Gladys could give. I learnt much from Lucia, but oh, how much more from my cousin Gladys!

After our bath Lucia introduced me to my own foutoir and bedroom. Like Gladys' it was a very handsomely adorned room, with books, pictures, ornaments and everything of a luxuriously and voluptuously erotic nature. There was the ottoman also, and well did I use it during the next few days. For our lovers soon heard of my arrival, and came running up to town to see and taste their new mistress. The ottoman was the consolatory article of those who could not immediately secure the night with me, or with Gladys, or with Lucia, and came into play almost every afternoon. I have sometimes given delight to four different admirers in the course of two hours! I loved it, but I loved my bed much better.

And what a bed! I had never dreamt of one like it. It was immense and delicious in every sense. It was a four-poster of the most solid mahogany, its posts being of extra strength to support a huge mirror which formed its canopy. Mirrors also, slightly inclined inwards, formed three sides of it, so that I could see every movement of my lover, whilst I felt his action and his power. And my lover, whilst lying by my side, could see my naked charms in front of him, or as it were suspended over him. So that not only had I the pleasure of being fucked, but I could enjoy seeing myself enjoyed, and, as Lucia said, it was indeed a fetching sight.

We sat down eight to dinner. I was introduced to Allan MacAllan and the other gentlemen, and although nothing very spicy was allowed in our conversation, we had a very merry party in which the very restrictions placed upon us made our wit all the more poignant.

By degrees I felt the ants crawling again. Charlie's prick had driven them away, but one fuck is by no means enough, and that a first one too. What added still more to the fire which consumed me was a small glass of some very delicate and delicious liqueur which we all partook of. It contained some powerful aphrodisiac, and I would have been better without it for I was burning. It took all I knew to prevent me making myself appear what I was, randy beyond anything I had ever felt.

But in Park Lane, we, though late sleepers, are early bed goers. At ten we said goodnight to the gentlemen and retired to our rooms. Annette came to assist me to undress, and when I was naked she produced my nightdress. What a dress! It was of some exquisitely fine and absolutely transparent silken material. It had no sleeves, but it fastened round my throat with a ribband which ran through eyelet holes. It was open from top to bottom, but fastened just above my breasts by ribands which were tied, and again below my breasts, across my waist at my hips, but so that the ribands hid none of my bush, and again, but more loosely, at my knees. Its utility as an article of dress was nil, but it greatly added to the attractiveness of my charms by just veiling them.

I had no sooner donned this elegant costume than Charlie appeared, and Annette, wishing us a goodnight, went off to prepare for her lover.

Oh, Charlie! No! My nightdress might be very fetching, but my naked skin was much more so. The moment he was naked, and he had stripped entirely, he untied all my ribbands, and there I was, as naked as himself.

Can I write down all the extravagancies of his behaviour – extravagancies which I, so far from finding outrageous, enjoyed to the uttermost? Ah, dear girls, dear readers, believe me, my pen fails me. What a night we had! What kissing, caressing, fucking! If I had enjoyed what Lucia called No. 1, oh! how I revelled in No. 2! What extra bliss there was in No. 3! How superlatively delicious was No. 4! And we did not end with No. 9, because we began again on waking, and completed No. 12!

After that Charlie acknowledged himself defeated! His proud prick begged for repose, and some time during the day he retreated to the country, having been, as he said, exhausted by the over-enjoyment of the naked charms of his charming cousin.

And so, dear reader, I come to the end of my story: she who knew nothing but sadness and loss found friendship and happiness, she who was all innocence and naivete gained knowledge and experience. The little country duckling became a beautiful town swan and thrived upon her new life in Park Lane.

Within a week of arriving I had enjoyed all the other men who had been present on the night of my maidenhead's ravishment. Oh, such fine, thick pricks they had! Such big, ponderous balls! Such abundant bushes! But none, no not one of them, could compete with the dear man who stole my virginity with such tender love: his wonderful, stiff warrior soon revisited the scene of his sweet conquest and, each time, he was eagerly received by my swollen, quivering quim, always ready to be fucked and filled and stretched to bursting point.

END

Thank you for buying this book – we hope you enjoyed it.

Why not get the 2nd Collection:

VICTEROTICA II

Made in United States
Orlando, FL
02 August 2022

20493426R00093